10-20

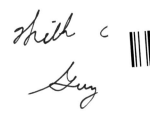
With a
Guy

D1555062

ACE CARROWAY
AND THE
GROWLING DEATH

GUY WORTHEY

ACE CARROWAY AND THE GROWLING DEATH

This is a work of fiction. Names, characters, places, and incidents are either the product of the author's imagination or are used fictitiously. Any resemblance to actual persons, living or dead, is entirely coincidental.

Cover design: Lauren Willmore

Copyright © 2019 Guy Worthey

ISBN: 1-949827-04-6
ISBN-13: 978-1-949827-04-0

 Westing Press

To Beecher Edmund Strube

For me, it is far better to grasp the universe as it really is
than to persist in delusion, however satisfying and reassuring.

— Carl Sagan

THE NEW YORK HERALD

COPYRIGHT, 1921, BY THE SUN-HERALD CORPORATION

NEW YORK, SATURDAY, NOVEMBER 5, 1921.—ENTERED AS SECOND CLASS MATTER,
POST OFFICE, NEW YORK, N. Y.

PRI

ESE PREMIER
BBED TO DEATH
EMENTED YOUTH

Attacks Statesman in Rail-
tation in Tokio and Is
ted, His Victim Dying
an Hour Later

EMIERSHIP IS ASSUMED
FOREIGN MINISTER UCHIDA.

ic End Will Not Upset Pro-
f Japan's Arms Delegation—
and Hughes Express Con-
ce—Baron Kato in Tears

(Associated Press).—Premier Hara was fatally stabbed
d the railroad station in Tokio. He died an hour later
of the station. The Premier was on his way to attend

SHIP BOARD ENTERS
ON ORIGINAL DUTIES
ABANDONED FOR WAR

Organization Never Has
Functioned as Originally
Was Intended.

NOW UNDER JONES ACT

Details of Fleet Corporation
Are Turned Over to New
Officials.

LASKER FINANCIAL HEAD

Various Bureaus Will Be in
Close Contact With I. C.
Commission.

Special Despatch to THE NEW YORK HERALD

GRISTLE GUS CAPTURED

WOMEN FLOATERS'
NEW VOTING MENACE

Seekers for Election Frauds
Find Suffragists Intrude
on Men's Preserves.

MANY CASES ON EAST SIDE

300 to 400 Illegal Registra-

HYLAN IS ASSAILED
AS A DUMMY MAYOR
AND TOOL OF HEARST

Curran Evokes Cheers by
Attack on City Adminis-
tration and Editor.

MAKES SIX SPEECHES

Says Home Rule Issue Is
Whether or Not City Shall
Be Run by 'Californian.'

TALKS IN HOME DISTRICT

Coalition Candidate Receives
Big Ovation From League
of Women Voters.

Before six cheering audiences in

HALF
SUPP
RIO

Police War
Violence h

F IFTY strik

Chapter 1

The goal was to see and hear without being seen or heard. The darkness in the observation room allowed the one-way mirror that covered most of one wall to function at its best. Black velvet instead of leather upholstered the wingback chairs, because leather creaks. Pleats and buttons smartly dressed sound-absorbing wall padding. Thick carpeting lushly covered the floor.

It was spying with class at C. Carroway & Associates detective agency.

The two men in the darkened room stood face-to-face with fists clenched, oblivious to their luxurious surroundings.

The slightly taller, dark-haired one said in clipped tones, "I didn't ask for your opinion, pretender! Besides, actors get paid to spout lies in front of audiences, so I couldn't believe you, anyway."

The blond man sniffed into the air in a gesture of dismissal. "I plead guilty to being a stage actor! You, on the other hand, are a lawyer! As such, you get paid *more* to lie in front of people who would rather hear the truth!"

A sardonic, nasal female voice crackled over intercom speakers. "Stifle! Here comes a client."

Both men whipped their heads to the large window (a window to them, but a mirror from the other side). In the neat, modern office beyond, Mrs. Figgins replaced the intercom handset in its cradle on the reception desk. She folded her hands with imperious dignity.

Her straight back and tight, gray-streaked bun complemented her acidic personality.

Beyond Mrs. Figgins's efficient cluster of file drawers, phones, desks, and typewriters, a cozy circle of couches and chairs abutted windows that let cloudy New York daylight in.

The two men whispered to each other, simultaneously.

"You started it, Bert!"

"You started it, Quack!"

"Bert" was Hubert Ewing Devery Christopher Bostock III, a young Boston lawyer.

"Quack" was Boxnard Warburton Snana. His neatly trimmed blond beard was left over from a recent run of Shakespeare's *Hamlet*, in which Quack played the title role. Back in the Great War, he had been a medic, but Bert called him a quack doctor and worked diligently to this day to keep the insulting title alive.

The men fell silent as the main office door opened. Both jaws grew slack, and all four eyes grew wide.

The svelte blonde slipped inside the door and hesitated. She cast an eye at the furnishings before focusing on Mrs. Figgins. Her hair swept boldly to one side, with a scarlet rose tucked above her exposed ear. The rest of her safflower cascade billowed artfully over her head and down the other side. Her cream chiffon dress was likewise asymmetrical. A splash of scarlet ribbon accented her left hip, and a right-side slit revealed a shapely calf as she walked.

"C. Carroway and Associates. How may we help you?" droned an unimpressed Mrs. Figgins. She turned away from her typewriter and reached for a steno pad.

"I really hope you *can* help! I've had a painting stolen. It's very valuable."

"Even her voice is beautiful!" whispered Quack, only to receive a cuff on the head from Bert in reply. They glared at each other for a second then gazed raptly through the window at the damsel in distress.

"Name. Address," said Mrs. Figgins in a monotone.

"Marilyn Murchison, 46 Bellevue Avenue."

"Did you call the police?"

Miss Murchison's wide eyes widened more. "Why, yes! But they won't listen to me. I have a clue, but they won't consider it!" She wrung her hands. "Will you take the case?"

With all the reluctance of a doomed pirate walking the plank, Mrs. Figgins said, "Have a seat. I'll ring an investigator." She chose one of several desk telephones and dialed a single number upon its rotary dial.

Marilyn Murchison exhaled in relief and perched on the very edge of one of the nearby stuffed leather seats. Mrs. Figgins spoke into the phone. "Marilyn Murchison. Stolen painting."

As the phone clicked into its cradle, a door opened at the far end of the office. Two men pushed through, jostling for first place. Bert won the race, and they abruptly slowed to a more dignified stroll. Bert straightened his tie. Quack smoothed his lapels.

Ignoring Mrs. Figgins's reproachful eye, they crossed to greet Marilyn Murchison. Bert offered a hand. "Greetings, madame! I am Hubert Bostock."

"Pleased to meet you, Mister Bostock." The young woman shook Bert's hand. She sent him a kittenish glance that might have contained a wink. Bert straightened and unconsciously sucked in his gut.

Quack looked anew at the blonde. Tones of wonder colored his rolling baritone voice. "Bless my soul! If it isn't Marilyn Murchison, recently the star of *Becky Sharp*, and before that a most exquisite Maid Marian in *Robin Hood*. I hope I am not mistaken."

Marilyn Murchison relaxed into a genuine smile. "Boxnard Warburton! What a pleasant surprise. Your name was on the marquee only last week. Are you really a private investigator by day?"

Bert turned amazed yet betrayed eyes upon Quack as the actor warmly enfolded Miss Murchison's soft hand in both of his. Quack chirped, "Yes, you could say that. And what puzzle have you brought us today? Something about a painting?"

"Oh, yes! My Pissarro is missing. I called the police, and they came, but they didn't want the best clue. This." The blonde opened her small handbag to produce a man's smoking pipe. She extended it toward Quack solemnly, as if it were of grave importance. "It wasn't there, before. But I found it on the mantel after. It must be the thief's!"

There was a moment of silence as Quack studied the carved pipe. He turned it over in his hands. He rubbed the back of his neck. "Well, the bowl part isn't wood. Is it rock? Rock with little bubbles?"

Bert crossed his arms. "A smoker. That narrows it down to about half a million New Yorkers."

"He's from Boston," Quack told Miss Murchison. "To him, New York is a barbaric nation somewhere to the south."

"Let me see that pipe," said a new voice.

No one had detected her approach. A simple flight suit with a wide belt and soft leather boots clad a tall, spare frame. Her calm, deep-hued face gave the impression of having been cast in metal by a master sculptor. Her gold-flecked eyes sparked with intelligence. Four long, parallel scars ran along her temple and cheek. She held out a hand toward Murchison. "Cecilia Carroway, at your service!"

"Ace! You gave me a start. How do you *do* that?" said Quack.

Miss Murchison put her hand in Cecilia Carroway's, alabaster on gold. Murchison conformed to the large-eyed, pale-faced popular ideal of New York beauty. In contrast, Ace could never land a leading lady role on Broadway. From short hair to boots and the leonine physique between, nothing about Ace approached the norm.

The actress gushed, "You're a woman! The 'C' is for Cecilia! I'm Marilyn Murchison. A pleasure, ma'am."

"Likewise, Miss Murchison." The pilot-detective took charge of the pipe, turning it this way and that. She addressed Bert, who stood with crossed arms and a frown. "Allow me to point out a few features of this pipe. Its owner is missing one of his lower teeth. See the extra gouges in the bottom of the stem? He rests it in the gap. No doubt it is quite comfortable. Also, he's a seafaring man."

Miss Murchison gasped. "Oh, but then my guess is right! I told a sea captain about my Pissarro just a few days ago! But how do you know that?"

Bert and Quack exchanged a quick, knowing glance. There would be a logical reason.

To the extent the tall woman's stoic, scarred face could be read, she looked more concerned than smug. "The pipe indicates exotic travel. There is no indication this was ever a retail object to be bought and sold. It is unique. The stem is ivory and carved with a monkey bas-relief in the style of Southeast Asia. Another feature is that the stummel is carved from a lightweight rock. This particular volcanic scoria has tiny, evenly distributed vesicles. Its origin is central Borneo."

"That's wicked specific," said Bert, eyebrows high. "You can tell by the bubbles?"

"And the density, light color, and peculiar toughness. I can't be absolutely certain. Similar volcanic deposits may exist in unexplored regions. But lumps of Borneo scoria are popular additions to mineral collections worldwide."

"My, my," said a wide-eyed Miss Murchison.

Wearing a grim expression, Ace handed the pipe back to her. "It's significant. These pipes are hard to make, and the tribes of Borneo are not interested in trade. They would never sell them to an outsider. Barring some extraordinary story, it stands to reason the current owner is a thief, or worse."

There was a brief moment of worried silence. Miss Murchison prompted, "Can you find him?"

"This sounds like the perfect case for us, Ace," Quack intoned. He kept his eyes carefully averted from Miss Murchison's figure.

"Right!" Bert said, his eyes fixated on her curves.

Ace flicked her eyes toward the omnipresent Mrs. Figgins and gave an affirmative nod. Figgins promptly droned like a nasal buzz saw, "Our standard contract is twenty dollars a day plus expenses. No guarantee of results. Carroway and Associates is not liable for any damages whatsoever. Sign here."

The actress seized the pen offered by Mrs. Figgins

and scribbled on the signature line.

CHAPTER 2

Ace gestured toward the exit door. "We might as well visit the scene of the crime. This sea captain you mentioned. What does he look like?"

Miss Murchison fell in step with the detective. "Oh, he was about Mr. Warburton's height but much thicker. He had bushy sideburns but no beard. Just a few gray hairs. I could believe he was a sea captain, with his weather-beaten skin and loud voice and all. I don't know if it means anything, but he had three bars on his coat sleeves. Maybe that's a rank or something. He didn't smile enough to show his teeth. His voice was a bit ragged. Gruff, you know."

"Can you remember a name?"

"I'm sorry, I don't remember his name! I don't know if he was with anyone. It was a crowded reception. Oh, I don't know!"

They descended the staircase from the third floor. The well-aged office building squatted at the intersection of Wall Street and Broadway.

"It might be enough. Did you take a taxi here, Miss Murchison?"

"Yes."

"All right. Let's drive my roadster. Sam parked it a block or two down."

Quack and Bert seemed to have invited themselves along. They jostled and pushed each other, but if Miss Murchison happened to glance their way, they feigned complete, smiling harmony.

Ace inquired, "What did this sea captain smell like?"

Bert blurted in surprise, "Smell? What does smell have to do with … ?"

But the actress seemed to find the question natural enough. "Not sea-breeze fresh! He smelled earthy, like a barn or, ahem, barnyard. Oh, and the shoulder of his coat was soiled with something light-colored. It could have been dirt."

Quack mused, "Or something smellier?"

"Could be, Mister Warburton," demurely answered the florally decorated blonde. Her sidelong glance at Quack quickened his pulse.

"Did he speak with an accent?" Ace placidly questioned as they arrived on the ground floor.

"Oh, yes! Something Eastern European. I remember trying to narrow it down as we spoke."

"You've a little hint of Central European slipping out now and then yourself, Miss Murchison." They emerged from the building's front doors onto the bustling street. "Well, that will be enough to start with, except for more details on the painting. It was original, I take it? By the way, here is my card."

As the tall, canvas-clad Ace held out a business card to the actress, several things happened.

First, a growl tore through the air. Not a growl like a dog, but a chilling, haunting growl that instantly brought a cold sweat and raised the hackles. It was enough to make anyone go pale, but pretty Marilyn Murchison blanched bloodless as the grating, low tones of the growl echoed and re-echoed over the street scene. Passersby halted in amazement and horror. Stare as they might, they saw no source for the primal, undulating cry.

As the unearthly growl reverberated, several metal canisters bounced toward Miss Murchison and the detectives on the sidewalk. The cans clanked and spun, and then erupted in angry hissing. Smoke gushed from the canisters. A stench like ammonia stung their noses as the air filled with gray-white vapor.

Ace dropped into a crouch, eyes roving.

Marilyn Murchison darted her eyes wildly here and there. She clutched at Quack's and Bert's elbows.

The doors on a sedan parked at the curb right in front of them popped open. Dark-clad figures emerged and raced toward them through the fog.

The smoke thickened fast. Sight distance shrank to inches. Shouts from fearful passersby confused the ear. Blocky bodies buffeted Bert and Quack. Miss Murchison's hold on them was broken.

She screamed.

A gravelly voice bit off, "Got 'er."

Bert cried, "Miss Murchison!" and lurched forward blindly, arms outstretched.

His hand brushed a moving figure, and he shouted, "Stop!"

The unseen figure did not stop but turned toward Bert. Bert felt an ill-aimed punch to his upper chest. "Aargh!" he blurted then cocked his own right arm back and let fly. His blow connected with something hard—a skull, by the feel of it.

Bert's adversary blared, "Surrender, by thunder!" accompanied by a solid punch to Bert's abdomen.

Bert's forehead wrinkled in pain and recognition, for the voice was Quack's. He doubled over and wheezed, "It's me, you idiot!"

A car motor revved. Tortured rubber squealed. Bert felt more than saw Quack swivel toward the sound and sprint away. Bert stumbled after, short on air after the gut punch. He gulped a lungful of acrid atmosphere, but it set him to coughing. When he reached the fringes of the spewing cloud, he caught sight of the receding car. Quack chased behind, almost at its bumper.

But Quack's heroic effort came a split second too late. The car accelerated away, and Quack gave up, arms windmilling and feet flapping. He spat a disgusted snarl and reversed course—and collided with Bert as the lawyer ran to catch up.

"Peon!" Quack ranted.

"Scab!" panted Bert back.

"Where is Miss Murchison? Where is Ace?" Quack demanded as he pulled Bert around and headed him back toward the scene of the attack.

A ring of timid bystanders shuffled about, talking, pointing, and gawking at inert gas canisters on the pavement. The artificial fog had thinned to tenuous wisps. A plumber picked up a business card from the sidewalk and squinted at it. Mystified, he read, "C. Carroway and Associates. Investigations."

Police sirens began to wail in the distance.

Bert replied in desolate tones, "They're gone!"

Chapter 3

Quack clapped both hands to his head and clutched at his own blond hair. "Both of them?"

Bert said, "I couldn't see a thing! But somebody grabbed Miss Murchison, so she's got to be in the getaway car, right?"

"I guess so. But I can't imagine Ace getting kidnapped so easily."

"True, but I can't think of where else she might be. Come on. We need the others."

Quack threaded his way through the loose ring of curious New Yorkers and grumbled, "It pains me to be forced to agree with you, you inkblot, but you're right. We need help. To the phone!" More loudly, Quack assured the crowd, "It's over. Nothing more to see here!"

Quack scooped up a spent gas canister from the sidewalk. He and Bert ran back to the detective agency.

At the moment the smoke filled the air and Miss Murchison screamed, the crouching Ace hugged low to the ground. The fog was thinner lower down. Avoiding the forest of legs, she padded catlike to the street to the rear of the parked car. It was a big one, a roomy Pierce-Arrow sedan with a rear trunk. Her strong, nimble fingers probed under her belt and extracted a metal tool that looked like a bottle opener. She felt along the rear trunk until she found the latch and keyhole. She thrust the tool under the edge of the trunk then ferociously twisted. The trunk popped open. In less than a second, it closed again with Ace inside.

Ace held the trunk open a crack and peered through. Most of the scene lay obscured in artificial fog, but away from the action, across the street, an unmoving figure stood. The thick legs and torso of a heavyset man seemed to support an enormous umbrella. Umbrella and man together traced a mushroom outline.

The car rocked as people piled in. Heavy people. Thumps and grunts sounded. A low voice barked, "Go." The 12-cylinder engine roared, and the car squealed off. Its doors slammed shut.

Ace lost sight of the man. And umbrella. But today's weather was rainless.

Ace squirmed in the cramped space, disturbing greasy rags. The smell triggered a memory.

Cecilia's linguistics tutor had fallen ill. The gleefully unobligated 13-year-old ran through the garden. She petted the flowers, cats, and stepping stones. She twirled a joyous pirouette. Her eyes fell on the detached car garage.

When her father found her before sunset, the entire drive train of the Model T was laid out, piece by piece, on the floor. His grease-covered daughter sat cross-legged with a wheel in her lap. Absorbed in concentration, she rolled the bearings around inside the cylindrical housing, her fingertips solid black.

"I'm torn between pride and irritation, Cecilia," Grant Carroway said, shaking his head.

She grinned up at him, teeth flashing white in the grease-

darkened face. "Choose pride, Dad! You know I'll put it back together. Is there any way we can cast iron? I thought of a better shape for the U-joint that won't leak as much grease." She tapped the driveshaft with a wrench.

"Cast? Iron?" Grant spluttered. Then he laughed. "Oh, very well, I'll see what I can arrange. But here's your price: put the car back together and get yourself scrubbed clean before dinner."

"Food tastes better when you're dirty," teased Cecilia. But she reassembled the wheels, axles, and driveshaft and, despite her words, managed a hasty bath, too.

In the cramped discomfort of the car trunk, Ace smiled.

Ace reached to her belt once more. She replaced her prying tool and extracted wire nippers. She twisted inside the cramped quarters to cut some wire out of the leads to the taillight. She wired the trunk to be cracked open by half an inch. She used a spare knee to hold the trunk lid so it did not flop.

She peeked out. The car raced northbound.

Male voices bit off tense words.

"Alley half a block ahead! Turn into it!"

"Gonna slow down. Gotta act normal. Don't want no coppers on our tail!"

"Stop squirmin', dollface, or I'll slug ya!"

Buffeted by the car's bumps and swerves and constrained by the small space, Ace about-faced with a hundred squirms. She applied her can opener again, this time on the metal between the trunk and back seat. She pierced the metal again and again then peeled a strip back.

The car dropped speed and joined traffic in a semblance of normalcy. Ace felt no swerves; the car still drove north. Traffic was light.

Ace resumed work on the back seat. Past the sheet metal lay a layer of thin wood. She worked slowly, keeping her splintering sounds of destruction under the roar of the Pierce-Arrow's engine.

"That's better, blondie. Behave an' we'll get along fine."

"Coppers! On the left!"

"Keep it cool. Keep it cool."

"They see us!"

"Keep it cool."

"No, they went the other way. Whew!"

"We're free! Head for the shack."

"Get yer foot off the gas! You wanna get pulled over now?"

As the sounds of other traffic diminished, Ace poked through fabric. She peeled back enough of the upholstery to get a peephole through the center of the back seat. Feeling like a contortionist, she strained her neck to scan all the angles. Four men. Directly below her eye, a woman slumped in the middle back seat. A band of cloth gagged her mouth. A heavy elbow in a frayed coat pressed her shoulder down below window level. Her cream chiffon dress splashed with blooms of red. After a stomach-churning second, Ace saw that the red splashes were not bloodstains. They were merely Marilyn Murchison's fashionable decorations.

Ace memorized what details she could glimpse of the four coarse, roughly dressed men. As she began the awkward twist process to face rearward again, a shard of metal poked her through her flight suit. The sharp pain, however inconsequential, brought Ace back to her girlhood.

Only the stars relieved the black of the African night. Little

Cecilia was alone. Her father writhed in the grip of malaria in a hospital hundreds of miles to the south. Langzaam, her guardian, lay crushed beneath his truck. Thinking her in safe hands, her Saan family wandered somewhere in the bush, as unreachable as the stars over Cecilia's head.

The girl herself stumbled on aimlessly through the brambles. Clotted blood crusted over a hundred cuts in her skin. Her bare feet flapped wearily, kicking up unseen dust with each exhausted step. But onward she must go. Any cessation of motion would bring them.

Them. The siafu ants. They would come again and climb her body. Without malice, each would lower their heads, open their powerful mandibles, and carve out a petite cube of her flesh. The ant would leave, carrying away its bounty, but it would be replaced by ten of its cousins. Cecilia was by now out of screams. She was out of tears. Only constant motion could save her.

But no motion is perpetual. Soon, thirst, hunger, or weariness would end the stalemate. The waking nightmare had but one possible ending.

Ace grimaced. She took a series of three calming breaths as required by the Wing Chun centering mantra. Her racing heart slowed. Her focus settled on the here. Her consciousness coalesced on the now, expelling the ghosts of the past.

Her lips twisted in a wry expression. "Someday, I'll feel an ant bite exactly at the wrong moment. I'll crash the plane. Or scream while hiding."

Curled in a position of relative comfort, she returned to observing their progress along the road through the crack between trunk lid and fender. The city blended to suburbs and then country.

Ace happened not to be wearing a radio pulse transmitter. If she were, her associates could track her by loop antenna. As it was, she could expect no help.

Time sped on.

She permitted herself the self-indulgence of a frown.

Chapter 4

Bert, the dark and handsome lawyer, stood on the street corner, fidgeting.

Quack, the blond, neatly-bearded actor, paced back and forth behind him. He glared at Bert's back frequently.

A low, smooth engine rumble pricked their ears. Their heads raised and swiveled expectantly. Moments later, a shiny four-door roadster braked to a halt in front of them with a screech and a puff of burnt rubber to wrinkle the nose. Despite the crisp November day, its windows were rolled down.

"Sam!" blurted Bert, "About time!"

The driver stroked his curled and waxed black mustache. "Sahibs, a thousand apologies if my arrival is tardy. I regret to announce that even frequent usages of the car horn did not move many New York drivers out of the way."

Sam Raia Biming's Egyptian ancestry showed in his umber skin, black hair, and brown eyes. Stuffed in the crack beside his seat, a manuscript on Coptic language and hieroglyphs gave away his career as an archaeologist.

Bert claimed the front passenger seat, and Quack piled into the back of the purring sedan. Even before the doors slammed shut, Sam raced the engine and popped the clutch. With another squeal of tortured rubber, the car leapt away.

"Ow, Sam!" Bert laughed as he bounced around the interior of the car. "Where'd you learn to drive like that?"

"Cairo, sahib. But what do you mean, 'like that,' Bert?" Sam took time to twirl his mustache with one hand then hastily clapped his hand back to the steering wheel to spin a sharp right turn.

"Yow!" The swerve threw Bert against Sam.

"Hey!" shouted a backpedaling New Yorker.

"Where are the others, Sam?" Quack braced himself by throwing an arm against the back of his seat.

"Very close, sahib."

Tire rubber complained once more as Sam braked without warning. Quack slammed into the back of Sam's seat, and Bert nearly cracked his head on the windshield. Before the rattling in their heads died down, the back door opened, and the car lurched to one side under a heavy tread.

"'Ello, one an' all!" Pale-skinned Phileas "Gooper" Locknard crammed his bulky self into the back seat. He winked a blue eye at Quack from under a bushy red eyebrow. His unkempt red mustache twitched. His bulging muscles made him resemble a circus strongman, but he was a field biologist by trade.

Quack found himself crushed between the massive Gooper and the car door. "Hey, Gooper, I like you and all, but—oh, I see. Here comes Tombstone."

A lanky, underfed collection of bones and sinew followed Gooper into the back seat. He folded his knees up almost to his chin and removed his Stetson. "Howdy, folks."

Tombstone slammed the door shut, and Sam

peeled out again, beaming a sunny smile as he managed, barely, to outrace an oncoming delivery van.

"Whoa, there, pardner." Tombstone's eyes widened.

Quack said, "It's all right. He learned to drive in Cairo."

"Cairo, ya say. Cairo? Ain't they even crazier there than Rome?" Gregory "Tombstone" Jamison's expertise lay in radio transmission and reception.

Quack felt something wriggle on his leg. He looked down. "Augh!"

A pair of beady red eyes blinked back. The pale-furred rat squirmed as it attempted to escape Gooper's tweed coat pocket. Gooper enfolded its tail in thick fingers and raised the rodent to eye level. The rat swung like a living pendulum as the racing car bumped and rocked.

Quack was vexed. "A rat? Gooper. Why?"

"'E seemed lonely, this *Rattus norvegicus*. Oi've named 'im Brownie." Gooper's mustache curved upward as he beamed at the animal. "Cootchie coo."

Tombstone said darkly, "Jes' keep him off *me*."

"Oi would never dream of slippin' 'im into anybody's cowboy boots, not me."

Tombstone and Gooper exchanged ominous glares. Quack rolled his eyes.

"Bert," Sam said.

Bert spoke through clenched teeth. "Yikes. We almost took the door off that car."

"Bert!"

"What is it, Sam?"

"Where do we go, sahib?"

"Oh. I have it written down." Bert fished in his

pocket and extracted a scrap of paper. "Murchison residence, 46 Bellevue Avenue, Long Island."

Seventeen angry honks and a bridge later, Sam slowed so that they could scan house numbers. Bellevue Avenue ran through spacious estates, manor houses, long driveways, and stone walls. The iron gate to number 46 was open. The roadster roared up the driveway past manicured shrubbery and hedges. Sam skidded the car to a halt at Grecian columns flanking the front door. The five piled out pell-mell, and Gooper rang the bell with nigh destructive energy.

Bert winced. "Gooper. Get back. Let me do the talking."

Gooper rolled shoulders that strained the seams of his coat. "As yew like it, guv."

A well-dressed manservant opened the fancy door and gazed out nervously at the five. They made an odd sight. Quack and Bert were slender men of average proportions in natty suits. Sam was short and stout in a waistcoat and cravat. Gooper was broad as a tweed barn, and Tombstone towered over the lot like a gangly scarecrow up a pole, dressed for a rodeo.

The butler recovered enough to say, "Yes? Can I help you?"

Bert inclined his head in courtly fashion. "We are with Carroway and Associates. Is this the Murchison residence?"

"It is." The butler relaxed enough to paste on a professional smile.

"Is she in?"

"No, sir. Would you like to leave a calling card?"

Gooper blew air through his ginger mustache. Brownie the rat scampered to his shoulder and wiggled its nose.

Bert shot Gooper a quelling glance then faced the butler with a grave expression. "This isn't a social call. We think Miss Murchison might be in some danger."

The butler blinked. His Adam's apple bounced. "Why do you think she is in danger?"

Behind taller men, Sam could not see well. But his ears detected the snap of a twig behind them. His companions apparently did not hear. He shot them an anxious glance, but they concentrated only on the butler.

Bert tried to break it gently. "There was an incident earlier today. Uh, involving the stolen painting."

"The painting? Oh, dear. Such a nasty surprise." He wrung his hands.

Sam gave up on attracting his associates' attention. He left the group and padded toward a hillock crowned with a manicured cluster of bushes.

"What painting was it? Who was the painter?" Quack said. Bert glowered at him.

"Oh, it was a picture of a village by the water by some famous Frenchman." The butler half-turned and pointed inside. "It hung there, in plain sight. Yesterday, we saw it was missing, and we called the police." The man broke off his speech. "Augh! What's that?"

It was a growl.

It was not at all like the growl of a dog, but a quavering, almost human ululation with gritty undertones that caused a wary stiffening in their spines. The backs of their necks prickled. The growl seemed to be everywhere around them, impossible to locate.

They darted glances in every direction, trying to locate the source of the eerie snarl. Only Sam could be seen, some distance away across the lawn. He pelted back toward them as fast as his short legs could carry him. Eyes bulging, he waved his arms and shouted, "Sahibs! Danger!"

In that moment, there was an odd illusion. Several dark objects, each trailing vapors, appeared to erupt from behind Sam's head. The dark metal tubes arced over Sam and clanged and ricocheted around the front doorstep.

"Grenade!" bellowed Gooper. He threw himself on top of the nearest. Brownie tumbled to the lawn.

Marilyn Murchison's manservant slammed the door and rammed the locks shut. Faintly, they heard him yelling from inside, "Police! Police!"

But the grenades were not explosive. They hissed, outgassing thin bluish vapors.

"Smoke bombs again?" wondered Quack. "But these don't … smoke … enough …" Quack's words slowed and slurred.

"Sam … what …" Bert gripped Sam's shoulders to halt the short Egyptian then blinked in slow motion as if his eyelids suddenly weighed pounds.

Gooper rolled off his grenade and opened his mouth to say something, but he yawned, instead. Moments later, he rolled onto his back. His bleary eyes closed, and he began snoring.

One by one, the associates crumpled to the ground.

Tombstone was the last to succumb. He turned to run, but the one lungful he inhaled was one too many. He tottered in a small circle then fell like a collection of dry sticks on top of his fallen compatriots.

CHAPTER 5

The shadows lengthened. Ace thought it must be approaching five o'clock. The Pierce-Arrow bumped over a rutted dirt track and finally crunched to a halt. The engine's twelve cylinders rattled to a stop. Breezes sighed, and a few birds called in the lonely fall-colored woods. The November evening air chilled the car trunk into an icebox.

"We're here," a gravelly voice announced.

"Get her in. Tie her to a chair," said a sharp-edged voice attached to a yellow shirt collar and the tendency to issue commands.

Ace unwrapped her wire holding the trunk cracked open and lightly held the trunk closed with her fingers. One of the goons might notice the slight damage or need to get in the trunk for something. Ace tensed her cramped body, ready for action.

The car doors opened. The Pierce-Arrow rocked as men climbed out. The mutterings of the four voices receded. A spring-loaded door creaked and slammed.

Ace stayed low as she rolled out of the trunk. Pins and needles shot through her cramped legs. She grimaced but stayed quiet as she beelined away from the car and shack.

She melted into the trees.

♠ ♠ ♠

"Beasts!" was the first word Miss Murchison was able to say as they finally removed her gag. Her hands and feet were bound with ropes to a chair. She gulped lungfuls of air, and her fear-widened eyes darted about. The shabby walls of the abandoned cabin enclosed moldy air. Four of the ugliest aberrations to ever populate a nightmare surrounded her, adding their unwashed funk to the ambient odor of decay.

"Shaddap!" said man with a scar across his eye socket and a yellow shirt. The gash of his mouth stretched between sneer and snarl. "There ain't nobody near to hear you scream, girly, but I don't like noise, see?"

"Jes' give 'er a drink, willya?" drawled a squat man with small eyes and droopy jowls. "Then gag her again."

"I don't want no water, but I could use a *real* drink right about now!" chuckled a chubby fellow whose round-cheeked smile did not reach his callous, uncaring eyes.

"When's Braun comin'? I want my pay," groused a weedy man in a tattered fedora.

Yellow-shirt reached out to whap the weedy one on the back of the head, causing his fedora to fall off. "You shaddap, too! You'll get what's comin', all right. We held up our end of the job. To perfection. Now, go fetch a glass of water. Go! Git!"

The weedy man picked up his hat then shuffled for the door, sending a sour squint to Yellow-shirt. "Yeah, yeah. I saw the pump. I'm goin'." The rickety spring-loaded screen door banged loudly as he left.

The actress trembled.

Yellow-shirt eyed her then shook his head side to side. "I got to wonder, though, if we ain't bein' shafted. Just think of the ransom we might get for this bit of skirt, eh?"

The jowly man grated, "Prison's full of kidnappers. The banks mark the money. Even if they don't get you at the payoff, they track you down when you spend it."

The jovial fat one smiled sunnily down at the helpless Miss Murchison. She shrank from him. A whimper escaped unbidden from her throat. The man's smile deepened.

Silence stretched for a minute. The three men shuffled, antsy. Finally, Yellow-shirt bellowed, "Rooney! Git in here!"

But only silence answered.

Yellow-shirt jabbed a finger at the jowly man. "Sudsy, go see if Rooney fell down a hole. Jeez. Get water, I said. Get water! It ain't complicated!"

The jowly one nodded and shuffled out the screen door.

A second after the door stopped banging, there came a choked cry then a heavy, wet thud sound.

"What the—" Yellow-shirt's jaw dropped. He made brief eye contact with the fat man, who no longer smiled.

Yellow-shirt's hand sprouted a four-inch knife blade. The fat man palmed a blackjack. They nodded to each other then flanked the door of the shack, one to each side, out of sight to any lurker outside.

The bound actress whimpered, her darting pupils wide pools of fear and misery.

Yellow-shirt glanced at her then simpered in well-greased tones, "Hey, who's out there? Come in so's we can talk, huh? No use bein' a stranger. Besides, we got a fun toy in here, oh yeah. Whaddya say?"

No one answered. Shine developed on the kidnappers' foreheads, and each rapid, shallow breath hissed.

And then, so suddenly it almost eluded the eye, a hand burst through the screen of the door. Lithe fingers hooked into the neck-flesh of the plump thug. The sinewy hand pulled. The fat fellow ripped through the screen, flailing. The flimsy, sagging door popped off its hinges, and the thug landed facedown upon its remains. In plain view of Miss Murchison, the tawny form of Ace Carroway dropped on the man, elbow first. The blow ended his movements.

Ace sprang back to a wide-footed stance, framed in the empty doorway about ten feet outside the shack. Her alto voice spoke one low and perfectly controlled word. "Surrender."

"What?" screamed the yellow-shirted ringleader. He charged out the empty doorway, knife raised. "Ain't no doll gonna—"

He slashed at the unarmed, motionless woman, his blade a silver streak.

His wrist met an unyielding metallic grip. The woman sidestepped and twisted the captured arm with brutal force. Face contorted in pain, Yellow-shirt whirled into the side of the shack, headfirst. The shack shuddered. Dirt sifted down from the ceiling into Miss Murchison's hair. The man bounced back and flopped in the dirt. He lay, feebly twitching. The golden apparition bent over him for a few moments, digging fingers into his neck with surgical precision. The man's twitching ceased.

"Ain't no doll … like Cecilia Carroway!" shakily observed Miss Murchison, half-sobbing the jest. "By golly, you're a sight for sore eyes!"

The fight-suited figure took Yellow-shirt's knife then strode inside to saw through the ropes at the actress's wrists and ankles. When the ropes fell, Ace crouched before the actress and gently massaged her bruised wrists.

"Marilyn. Did they knock you on the head at all?"

"No. They gagged me to keep me quiet."

"You look like you're in one piece. Just frazzled."

"And you haven't even mussed your hair! That was amazing!"

"My hair comes pre-mussed. Saves time. Do you know who—wait. What is that sound?" The crouching woman raised a few inches taller. Her head veered this way and that, questing. Ace crept toward what was once the kitchen, sinking lower.

Miss Murchison rose from the chair and wobbled on trembling legs. "I don't hear anything."

"Shh. It's ticking."

Ace crept toward the cabinet under the rusted, useless sink. She reached out to touch the warped, neglected wooden flap. Carefully, slowly, she opened the cabinet door. The ticking grew louder.

Both women beheld the machine inside, transfixed. It was composed of a pyramid of canisters topped with wires and a ticking timer. With a strained titter, the battered stage star said, "If I didn't know better, I'd say that was a bomb."

Chapter 6

In a flash, Ace spun and sprinted. Ace planted her shoulder into Miss Murchison's midsection and heaved her up and out the door. "About to blow!" she bit off as they hit the free air.

Miss Murchison flopped like a sack over Ace's shoulder. Breathless, with the wind knocked out of her, she wheezed, "Wha—? A bomb? A time bomb? Who? How? Why?"

The blast caught them a few car lengths past the Pierce-Arrow. A piston of solid air swatted them forward. They hit the ground and tumbled heels over head. Half stunned, ears ringing, Ace scrambled to shield the actress with her own body. Debris rained down for a quarter minute that felt like an eternity.

Finally, they sat up and exchanged cautious glances. The left shoulder of Ace's flight suit lay in tatters, though the burnished skin underneath seemed unmarked. The pilot-detective gazed back toward the smoking mound of detritus. Nothing more remained of the hut. Only shattered heaps of rubbish mounded where the three unconscious men had lain. From low in Ace's throat throbbed a warbling hum, entrancing and otherworldly. Her gold-flecked eyes focused far away, and her lips pursed in contemplation.

"Can you hear me?" wondered Miss Murchison aloud.

"Well enough," Ace said with a lopsided smile.

"Bengt Braun. That is his name. One of the men just now said it, and I remembered. But I still almost don't believe it! He meant to … to …."

"Kill you," Ace finished curtly. "Along with his hirelings."

The blonde woman's face seemed drained of all blood, so pale it grew. She said, "I must believe it, then. I must! He's a monster!"

"The lives of others mean little to this man." Ace's tone could freeze water.

"But you. You are the opposite. You risked your own life to come after me." Marilyn's eyes searched Ace's in incomprehension.

Ace squirmed and changed the subject. "That Pierce-Arrow might still be drivable. It would be smartest to drive to a phone and call for help."

Murchison continued to stare at Ace. "Why do your men call you Ace?"

Ace rose to her feet and tugged Murchison up. She sighed. "I was a double ace in the Great War."

"What? You can't have been. I mean, surely I'm older than you are."

"Marilyn. We should save story time for later."

"You're right. I'm all for getting out of here!" They inched cautiously toward the Pierce-Arrow.

Ace frowned anew at the scene of utter annihilation. Lines creased between her brows, and she asked Murchison sharply, "Is this really about paintings of the old masters?"

Blue eyes widened then darted side to side. Not meeting Ace's gaze, she said glibly, "Yes. Yes, of course. My fortunes have slipped of late. My bank account is empty. All I have left of value is my art collection."

"You're in need of cash."

"Yes. Yes, I am."

There was a brief silence. Ace said, "Do you happen to own a Degas or a Monet?"

Night fell. At the corner of Wall Street and Broadway, an impeccable four-door roadster coasted to a stop behind a shattered, abused Pierce-Arrow. Five men emerged stiffly from the shiny roadster to gather in a silent semicircle around the hulk. None of its glass was more than jagged fragments, two tires were rags of rubber around the rims, it was covered in dents, and patches of the paint seemed to have been burned. It was missing one door entirely, and the trunk flapped loose.

"What th' heck? It looks like it's been firebombed!" said Tombstone.

Quack massaged his temples and murmured, "If my head didn't hurt so bad right now, I think I'd bash it on the wall or something. Please tell me that's not the getaway car."

"It's the getaway car," Bert murmured back.

"How can it be?" Quack moaned.

"How did it get here?" said Bert.

Tombstone answered, "With a lotta bumps. Lookit them tires blown out."

A cab pulled up next to them. The cabbie whistled with appreciation. "Those two cars! Beauty and the beast! Ha! Ha!"

"Oh, haw, haw. I'm goin' ter ignore your anomalistic ebullience, hack!" said the apelike Gooper. His custom was to dredge the depths of the dictionary for vocabulary then mangle the flowery words with an English Cockney of the most guttural sort.

The cabbie killed his engine and adjusted his cap. He levered open his door and got out.

Gooper brightened up. Maybe the fellow was spoiling for a brawl. Certainly, a straight fight would be more satisfying than getting gassed *en masse* and sleeping away the twilight on the Murchison lawn.

But the cabbie just lounged against his own double-parked vehicle and clucked his tongue at all the damage done to the Pierce-Arrow.

The wrecked car fascinated them. Even the rat poked a pulsating nose out of Gooper's coat pocket to survey the destruction.

Finally, Bert asked the cab driver, "Say, why are you here?"

"To pick me up!" answered a bright soprano behind them.

Five heads swiveled as one. A female form emerged from the glass doors of the building lobby.

"Miss Murchison! What a relief to see you," Quack said. The actress wore a flight suit with cuffs rolled up to shorten the sleeves and pant legs. Her hair fell in a simple, well-brushed glossy cascade.

From the door behind her, a taller figure stepped.

"Lady Ace!" Sam cried.

"I'm so glad you're all right!" said Bert.

"Both of you!" said Quack. "I felt so powerless! That horrible growl sound, and then you were both gone! Turned to smoke, like Coyote the trickster."

"Cor! Lookit them peepers!" Gooper said dreamily,

smiling vacantly at the actress.

"Where are yer British manners." Tombstone nudged Gooper. "Ya homely Limey."

Sam bowed from the waist. "I take it that you are the Miss Murchison we were chasing? Indeed, it gives pleasure to know that you are alive and well and unharmed."

"What charming gentlemen. Perhaps the age of chivalry isn't all the way dead. I've had better days, for sure, but it turned out well at its end." She pivoted. "Ace, I don't think I'll ever be able to thank you enough."

The tall woman's lips twitched. "Don't try. Your cab awaits. I'll call about noon tomorrow, and we can make the exchange. Good night, Marilyn."

The actress laughed. "As you like it!" She skipped over to the cab. The driver handed her into the back seat. She rolled the window down and called, "Good night, boys! Good night, Ace!"

"Gotta love New York!" the cabbie said with a wink. He restarted his engine and puttered off down the empty street.

Ace narrowed her eyes as she inspected the row of five haggard faces and five sets of rumpled clothing. "What happened to *you*?"

Tombstone's long face resembled that of an undertaker even more than usual. "Gas attack, ma'am. Knocked us all out for over an hour."

Sam smoothed his curled mustache. "We were at the Murchison manor, memsahib. Several masked men approached the house, but my shout of warning came too late."

Quack shook his head from side to side. "Not all

the way too late. The butler stayed safe inside the house."

"He musta called the poe-leece," Tombstone said.

Sam nodded vigorously. "We came to consciousness with policemen slapping our faces. The masked men left no traces."

"You forgot the growl," Bert said. "The same horrible sound as when Miss Murchison disappeared."

Ace tapped her chin. "Did the gas smell like ether?"

Quack rubbed his forehead. "Maybe. Memory's a little fuzzy."

"I see." Ace's eyes fell on Gooper, and her eyebrows worked. She winced as if fearing the reply but forged ahead. "Gooper, explain the rat."

Gooper's mustache curved upward and bristled proudly. "'Is name's Brownie. Innee a darlin'?"

"You took him from a research lab?"

Gooper rubbed at the base of his skull, which sat directly on his shoulders without a visible neck. "Rescued, m'lady, rescued, not absconded wif. But wot 'appened to yew, me unparagoned amazon? 'Ow did yew rescue Miss Murchison?"

"And what happened to this car?" Quack gestured to the junked Pierce-Arrow.

"I'll tell you when we have free time, but right now we have detective work to do. If you're feeling up to it."

All five straightened up.

"Oh, yes, memsahib!"

"Time ter dive inter the ruck?"

"I'm as frisky as a colt in spring."

"Bring on the slings and arrows of outrageous fortune."

Bert added, "Count me in, too. What's up, Ace?"

Ace grinned big at the chorus of affirmatives. "We're going to burn a little midnight oil tonight. Tombstone, take Gooper and the van. Set up a listening post off Bellevue Avenue. Tap the Murchison manor's telephone. Take care to see if anybody is watching the place. We'll reconnoiter at your post tomorrow, probably about eleven o'clock. Ring up Mrs. Figgins when she gets in. Copy?"

The men nodded briskly. Ace signaled thumbs-up and swiveled to her next targets. "Bert and Quack, hit the library. See what you can dig up about a seafarer named Bengt Braun. Possibly a ship captain. Probably from Eastern Europe. Perhaps military for a while, with the Ottoman navy as first guess. Got all that?"

They, too, nodded crisply. Ace pivoted. "Sam, you and I will check Marilyn Murchison's history. There's more to her than the pretty face she shows us."

"Of course, Lady Ace," Sam replied with a neat bow.

"Wheels up!"[1] Ace called, and the six scattered, bright minds united in a common goal.

---

[1] The command "wheels up" derives from recent aviation advances. The newest airplanes retract their landing gear when fully airborne to reduce drag and increase lift.

CHAPTER 7

Gooper and Tombstone drove a van packed with tools and electrical gear to the neighborhood of the Murchison residence. With the memory of fizzing gas grenades fresh in their minds, the two men examined every shadow, but the neighborhood seemed quiet. They parked the van in front of a telephone pole. Tombstone donned spike boots, tool belt, and a lumberjack harness and shimmied up the pole. A few minutes later, a coil of zip-wire dropped from on high down to Gooper's waiting hands. Tombstone worked his way back down again, tacking the dangling wire to the pole. Gooper fed the wire into the van and twisted the ends to terminals on a box encrusted with dials and knobs.

They closed themselves into the van and began the tedium of eavesdropping on the telephone calls to or from 46 Bellevue Avenue.

Meanwhile, Quack, Bert, Ace, and Sam scoured their private library on the secret 4th floor of their Wall Street and Broadway office. When they could glean no more information, they scattered. Ace examined criminal records at the police station (her recent success bagging the Smugglers Crossroads gang had made her popular downtown[2]). Quack got on the horn to request information from the Naval Secretariat. Bert visited the League of Nations building. Sam went to the public library to trace Miss Murchison's acting career.

Late next morning, the researchers groggily reconvened, only to be shepherded into the roadster by Ace. She raced to the bank. Ace screeched to a halt and leapt out.

"Did she get more sleep than us, or does she just not need sleep?" said Quack as he rubbed his sandy eyes.

"Assuredly, she is the fox among the mongrels," Sam said.

Bert woozily inquired, "Um. Does anyone know why we are at the bank?"

No one did, but it became evident when Ace returned, carrying a stuffed envelope. She plopped it on Quack's lap. "Count that, please."

Ace slipped behind the wheel, and Quack unwrapped a chunky wad of folding green. Quack whistled a glissando of wonder. "Shopping spree money?"

Ace's enigmatic half-smile was her only answer.

On Bellevue Avenue, Ace throttled the roadster down to a rumbly purr and a sedate speed.

Quack reported, "I make it two thousand, two hundred dollars. What gives, Ace?"

Ace replied, "Tell you in a minute. I see the radio van." The familiar van sat curbside down a cross street. Ace meandered another block further and parked. Walking in pairs so as to be inconspicuous, the

---

[2] The full story is related in *Ace Carroway and the Handsome Devil.*

whole crew soon enough arrived inside the listening post.

"Salutations, compatriots!" Gooper and his ginger mustache beamed at them. Inside the van, drawers full of vacuum tubes, resistors, capacitors, bulbs, magnets, and inductors competed for space with antennae and spools of wire. The addition of six people cramped the remaining space, especially since Gooper bulked double a normal human.

"Any phone calls?" Ace asked.

Tombstone answered, "Yep, two. Number one was to a Mister Norbert Funkenhausen, an art dealer. Miss Murchison asked that he come at noon to oversee a sale." Tombstone's suspicion leaked out in his West Texas drawl. "Seems a certain Ace Carroway is comin' t' buy a Day-gah painting."

"'E means Degas, the Frenchie painter," Gooper translated. Gooper squinted at Ace. "So? Is it true?"

Ace wiggled her eyebrows. "Perfectly true. We can't talk too long, or I'll miss my date."

"It explains all the money you withdrew," Bert said.

Ace said, "And number two?"

Tombstone replied, "Number two was incoming, from the poe-leese. They wanted our Miss Murchison downtown fer a positive identification on her kidnapper and a general statement of what happened. What *did* happen, Ace?"

Ace said, "I'll give you the short version in a minute. Sam, what can you tell us?"

Sam's precise consonants defined his report. "I can tell of steady success for the actress Marilyn Murchison, at least in these last few years after the end of the Great War. She began auditioning on Broadway and has had steady work. Before that, it is confusing. One story is that she escaped from an Ottoman prison. One story is that she was born in Kansas, but the next has it that she was born in Prague. But she did not arrive in New York poor. She was rich enough to buy the house she still occupies. Her art acquisitions came later and gradually, and she is now a well-known collector. I am troubled by how hard it is to find out anything about her earlier years, Ace."

"Interesting. Thank you, Sam. As for me, I discovered that she has no criminal record, at least not in New York. She has been the subject of a scandal or two, about the same as any Broadway belle. Perhaps most interesting, I found her immigration record. She was an Austrian citizen when she arrived in America. Oddly, though her last name is Murchison, she listed her deceased parents as having the last name Heber. What sprang to mind was the Ottoman minister of the interior, Ernst Heber, but one mustn't jump to conclusions."

"Ernst Heber!" Quack blurted. "If she's his daughter, she played it smart by staying quiet about it! She would make no friends on this side of the pond by bragging on *that* daddy!"

"It is suggestive, not proven," Ace said flatly. "Quack, what did you discover about Bengt Braun?"

"I discovered that Braun is an extremely common name, for one!" grumped the blond actor. "There were three Captain Brauns and one Admiral Braun in the Ottoman Navy. But one of the captains and the admiral died with public funerals, so we can scratch them off the list right away. One Captain Braun had the first initial 'K,' and he saw action mostly on the Red Sea and Indian Ocean. The other Captain Braun had the first initial 'B' and captained supply ships on the Mediterranean."

Quack tapped the side of his nose. "It occurs to me that during the Great War, supply ships would have been organized under …."

"… Minister of the Interior Ernst Heber," Bert finished for him.

Ace shot Bert a quelling look. "Bert, your turn. Speculation aside, what *concrete* things did you dig up?"

Bert cleared his throat. "Right. My assignment was Bengt Braun. I found two international arrest-and-extradite warrants, both for a dark-haired man named Bengt Braun. One is for theft in Goa, India, four years ago. The other is for theft in Djibouti, two years ago. If it's the same guy, he gets around."

Ace was silent for a moment, then her controlled voice summarized, "There is a lot we do not know. The strange growling sound, for one. I have never heard its like before."

"Such a sound fills the soul with dread." Sam shivered.

Ace said, "It may mean nothing, but as Miss Murchison was being kidnapped there was a man across the street. He was a thickly built fellow and carried a very large umbrella."

Bert and Quack glanced at each other then at Ace. "But it wasn't raining," they said in unison.

Ace said, "Precisely. Odd. But I can make nothing of it. Moving on, the police are tracing the gas canisters, but they looked like Ottoman surplus to me, in which case the police will get nowhere.

"Bengt Braun is a habitual thief, and I'd give 99

percent odds he's a murderer, too. He hired four local musclemen to kidnap Miss Murchison and take her to a rendezvous in the woods. They delivered her there, and I hitched a ride in the car trunk. My plan was to take the leader in for questioning, but I didn't get a chance. I found a bomb on a timer, and it was all I could do to get Miss Murchison out of range before it blew."

Tombstone whistled. "A bomb! So that's what banged up that getaway car?"

Ace said, "Yes, that's right."

"Well, tan my hide an' call me leather!"

Gooper poked Tombstone with a burly elbow, and Ace continued while they exchanged glares. "Only one of the thugs survived in good shape. He's in custody. Two are in the hospital. One is dead. If I hadn't been there, all five of them would've perished. I think we can safely assume that Bengt Braun wanted to erase Miss Murchison along with her kidnappers."

Quack twitched in agitation. "But, but then he might try again once he knows he failed!"

Ace said, low and grim, "He very well might, and that's why we are keeping such close tabs on Miss Murchison right now."

With a lighter tone of voice, the flying ace shifted gears. "Tombstone?"

"Yup?" drawled the cadaverous electrical engineer.

"After my visit, if my guesses are right, Miss Murchison may find sudden interest in her telephone. Get ready to take good notes."

"Will do!"

Ace reached for the van door handle. "Quack, come with me. Everybody else, set a watch and keep

Tombstone company."

Bert huffed. "Why Quack? I'm available!"

Quack smirked. "Better luck next time, Romeo."

Chapter 8

Marilyn Murchison's man ushered in Quack and Ace. "Are you recovered, sir?" he asked Quack.

"Yes. Thanks to you, I understand."

"Oh, no, sir. The police were very prompt, sir."

Ace said, "Did you ever hear a growl like that, before?"

"No, madam." The butler's face tinged a shade grayer.

"Did you see anybody's face?"

"Madam, you overestimate my courage. I did nothing but call the police, and I did that from beneath Miss Murchison's bed. I saw nothing. Do come in."

Ace and Quack stepped from the red-carpeted hallway into the library. The butler called, "Visitors, mistress."

The actress flowed to meet them in an orange-brown full-length sleeveless dress. "Oh, hello! Come in, come in! How nice to see you, Mr. Warburton!"

"The pleasure is mine, Miss Murchison." Quack captured her outstretched hand and tickled her knuckles with his Hamlet whiskers.

"To business, please." Ace's mouth was a thin line.

Murchison and Quack dropped their hands and snapped up straight.

"Of course, Cecilia. This way." Murchison gestured around the wood-paneled library and sitting room. The polished walls held many paintings and one bare spot. She led her visitors to a painting on the wall two spac-

43

es to the left of the missing one. The Degas canvas depicted a trio of ballet dancers stretching on the barre, dressed alike in blue leotards and tutus.

A short, white-haired man leaned on a cane in front of the painting. He squinted through pince-nez at Ace and Quack.

"This is Mr. Norbert Funkenhausen," Murchison said. "These are Cecilia Carroway and Boxnard Warburton."

Funkenhausen mumbled a greeting then resumed rapt contemplation of the painting.

Their hostess gestured grandly to the oil painting. "I present to you *Dancers in Blue.* I think about half of Degas's work was done in a dance studio. Isn't it just—evocative?"

"It is indeed. Serene yet energetic. Beauty, but beauty in motion," Quack agreed, though his glance strayed to the actress more than the painting.

Ace stayed silent for a long while in her perusal of the painting, gold-flecked eyes seeming to bore beyond the surface of the painted canvas. Her glance flicked to Miss Murchison, who wrung her hands. Ace said, "I offer two thousand, two hundred."

Quack blew air into his cheeks. Norbert Funkenhausen didn't bat an eye.

Quack studied the blonde actress. He thought her facial expression looked not really happy or unhappy but *resolved.* She nodded. "All right, as long as you have cash."

"I do. It's what I brought with me, no more, no less. I wasn't going to haggle." Ace handed the bank envelope to Miss Murchison. "Please. Count it."

And so the deal was sealed. Funkenhausen's briefcase disgorged paperwork to shuffle and a seal to notarize the signatures. Funkenhausen and the butler helped Quack pack the painting in a sturdy box. The women supervised from a nearby table and sipped tea. Miss Murchison enjoyed a game where she let her bare ankle show then counted Quack's glances.

Ace tried some leading questions but made no dent in the actress's poise. After farewells, Quack hefted the box from manor house to roadster.

As they drove the two blocks to the vicinity of the listening post van, Quack tapped a finger on the crated painting. "I've heard of Degas. The painting seemed original to me, though I'm sure I couldn't tell it from a copy."

"It is original. It would sell for more than I paid at an art auction. I got a deal."

"I didn't know you were an art collector, Ace."

"Mm? Oh, I'm not."

"Really? Then why did you buy the painting?"

"Because Miss Murchison will not tell me the whole story, but I think she told the truth about being out of funds. In order to get more of the story, I provided some funds."

Quack's brow furrowed. "She needed cash quick. And a crooked sea captain wants her dead. I don't like this, Ace."

When Ace and Quack arrived back at the mobile listening post, Tombstone had his head down, scribbling like a madman on a paper tablet. With his free hand, he jammed a little loudspeaker against his ear. Gooper took charge of the inked-up sheets ejected by the Texan writing machine. Gooper scanned them, a blunt finger moving under scrawled lines of cursive.

"Assuredly, yer handwritin' would grievously disappoint yer teachers, Tombstone," he jibed. He crowed to Ace and Quack, "She's buyin' a bulldozer from Acme Heavy Industries!"

Bert philosophized, "A fine woman turns fine art into fine machinery."

Quack replied with some heat, "Oh, stop. She's fine, all right. Too fine for the likes of you, shyster!"

Bert started to reply, "You fake little—" but Gooper reached out a thick hand and placed it firmly over Bert's mouth.

"Shut it, mate." Gooper waved the sheet of Tombstone's latest scribbles. "She's charterin' a transatlantic ship!" Gooper squinted at the sheet and frowned, causing his bushy red walrus mustache to frown, too. "Mediterranean Sea … Sius? They're going ter Sius."

For a brief span of time, there was an otherworldly, omnipresent humming sound, hypnotic and warbling. The men stared at Ace until her eyes focused on the here and now and the entrancing hum faded. Five pairs of eyes stared at her, owlish in the dim light.

She snorted in amusement at the sight. "Well, I didn't expect Sius."

Sam breathed reverently, "Sius! It would be a privilege to walk upon its legendary shores."

Bert eyed Sam in the gloom. "Catch me up. I vaguely remember that Sius is a volcanic island. And I think maybe uninhabited. What do you know that I don't?"

Sam traced a finger along the curl of his mustache. "The volcano Sisuvius appears in the legends of every past Mediterranean civilization, sahib. Homer named it Scylla in *The Odyssey* because passing ships run afoul of rock outcrops and sink. Also, ships are sunk by cinders tossed by Sisuvius as it erupts."

Ace picked up the narration. "Geologists and photographers study the red basalts that stain the volcano like rivulets of blood. Left in the weather for too many years, the bright red color fades, but the fresh lava flows are a dramatic crimson color. Chemically, it's probably elevated proportions of iron and carbon."

"Blood mountain," Sam said in hushed tones.

Ace pursed her lips. "Worth mentioning is that about a century ago, a ship transporting African animals ran aground on Sius, and its cargo escaped. I've heard rumors that Ottoman big game hunters visited there to hunt before the war."

Quack shook his head back and forth, marveling. "How do you know all that, Ace?"

But Quack knew the literal answer. Ace's father, millionaire Grant Carroway, had spared no expense in educating his only child. Only the brightest in each field of human endeavor tutored young Cecilia. Ace picked up her own education where her father had left off. She traveled widely and consulted experts in fields as diverse as metallurgy and astronomy, linguistics and ballistics, oceanography and radioactivity.

"Keep listening, Tombstone," Ace said. "Bert. Sam. When we get to the office, take Bert's car and head to the hangar. Make sure the collapsible airship and the hydrogen-extraction gear are in their crates and ready to ship."

"Airship. Check," said Bert.

"It will be our pleasure, Ace," Sam enunciated happily.

The eyes of all six shone bright. And why not? Mystery abounded. The air buzzed with the possibility of a chase. The meaning of the chilling growl was unknown except for one thing. It meant danger.

Chapter 9

The next day, the case advanced in three ways.

First, Miss Murchison visited Acme Heavy Industries in Newark to inspect a tractor. She was shown to the line of small excavators and bulldozers by a gruff, bent, squint-eyed mustachioed man who said his name was Wizenby. The man's real name was not Wizenby, but he was a good salesman.

"A powerful tractor, but not too tall," Murchison said. She fiddled a lot with her ring. She shot glances at nearby tractors and trucks as if they might pounce.

"What jobs will it do?" Wizenby asked, daring only brief glances at the spectacular young woman.

"It will pull boulders. I guess I need chains."

Wizenby pointed out a modest-sized Allis-Chalmers with caterpillar treads. It had a rear claw for pulling boulders and a front blade for pushing. Wizenby was barely started on extolling its virtues when she interrupted.

"I'll take it." She requested to have the dozer and extra fuel delivered to Pier 71 before noon the following day. Wizenby fetched his supervisor to finish the paperwork, and the transaction was completed.

After Murchison departed, Wizenby straightened up taller than he had been the last hour. He turned to his supervisor and spoke in a voice suddenly full and powerful, and not gruff at all. "Thank you, Mr. Templeton. As 'Wizenby,' I'll deliver the tractor tomorrow." Wizenby then peeled off his theatrical prop mustache. "Plus, I got a few more clues about what might be going on in this mystery!"

Templeton shrugged, his eyes crinkling merrily at the corners. "I sure didn't lose out, Mr. Warburton. She paid full price for that tractor *in cash*. And I got to see you pull off some amazing character acting."

"Heh. I was nervous, tell you what. She knows my face. It would've been awfully awkward if she'd recognized me, and I'd really hate explaining the goof-up to Ace."

Templeton grinned. "I'd do anything for Ace Carroway. I was in the crowd the day she landed that giant Ottoman airship right in Piccadilly Circus. I'll never forget that. I cheered until my lungs wore out."

Quack laid a hand on Templeton's shoulder in a moment of accord.

The second step forward in the case began when Mrs. Figgins answered a phone call from the police station.

"C. Carroway and Associates, investigations," she droned.

"This is Detective Holloway. Is Ace around? I got news," came the tinny, clipped tones over the phone.

"She's right here," Mrs. Figgins said grumpily. The police were one category of callers she could not abuse.

Ace picked up the phone. "Yes, detective?"

"Nice to hear your voice, Miss Carroway. You

know that bird you tied up for us in the woods? When we told him all his buddies were dead or at death's door, he sang like a second Caruso[3]. He told us where to find this Braun guy. We sent guys over there a minute ago, but I thought you'd wanna know, too."

"I do! Where?"

"It's a dump at 141 Howard in the Bronx."

"I'm on my way. Thanks, detective! I owe you a box of cigars."

The detective opened his mouth to reply, but there was a click on the other end of the line. He shook his head from side to side and clucked his tongue. "She's fast. I'd give even odds she'll beat the patrol cars there."

Not many minutes later, Ace, Gooper, and Sam screeched to a halt behind a pair of police cruisers and swarmed out to a quiet scene. A few officers poked around a tenement. It was shabby, unkempt, dark, and silent. A lieutenant chatted with neighbors nearby. Spotting Carroway and her associates, he sauntered over. "Braun's gone. Didn't pay his last month's rent, and cleared out. Nobody around here spoke to him much. He kept to himself. He entertained quite a few rough characters. That's all we got."

Gooper and Sam's faces fell. The golden-haired flying ace, however, seemed to take it in stride. "Thank you, lieutenant. What sort of car did he drive?"

"A rusty Studebaker. Common as mud, sorry to say. There must be a hundred others like it in the city."

"Disappointing. Anything else?"

---

[3] Celebrated tenor Enrico Caruso specialized in French and Italian opera and made many early recordings.

The officer placidly nodded. "His trash was full of empty tobacco tins and banana peels. You could smell the tobacco in the house, along with other stink. Deadbeat pigs." The lieutenant spoke without much feeling. Dealing with the unsavory was part of the job.

The tall woman nodded. "Fair enough. We know he smokes a pipe. Lieutenant, one more question. Did the neighbors hear any—growling?"

The policeman blinked. "Yeah, that lady there was just trying to describe the growls. Apparently, they made quite an impression. She was scared to go outside."

Sam and Gooper exchanged glances, eyebrows raised. Their mustaches twitched.

"What?" the policeman asked, looking back and forth between them.

Gooper rumbled, "We've 'eard th' growling b'fore."

♠ ♠ ♠

The third case advancement occurred when Bert burst into the office in the early evening.

"Too late!" He moaned.

"What's too late, you overdramatic stuffed shirt?" Quack wondered. His beard was gone, sacrificed for the sake of Wizenby the tractor man.

"Oh, shut it, you blight. The Pissarro painting sold in D.C. at an auction today. The seller already got his cash." Bert's expression resembled a man forced to drink sour milk. "The auction house refused to tell me anything about the buyer. Nothing. They got all huffy.

Phooie."

In polite tones, Sam suggested, "We could beat it out of them."

There was a conversational pause. Every eye swiveled to the Egyptian archaeologist. Finally, Tombstone drawled, "Ya feelin' feverish, son?"

Sam stuttered, "I, I, I am apologetic. My mouth has run like water down a hill."

Gooper grinned. "Bloke's got a hermetic yen fer th' altercation, methinks!"

Ace's eyes sparkled with amusement as she patted Sam on the back.

Quack said soberly, "The painting sold, so now Bengt Braun has a lot of cash?"

Ace said, "It would seem so."

Tombstone scowled. "Ah hate t'think what th' dirty buzzard's gonna buy with it."

"Something more than maps and a compass, I presume," Ace said. "Speaking of travel, I had difficulty finding a ship. Nothing from Carroway Shipping is anywhere near the eastern seaboard right now. However, I talked to the captain of a tramp steamer called the *Diving Loon*. He was happy to accept the extra commission for passengers and our crates containing the balloon. Miss Murchison, on the other hand, has commissioned the *Sea Leopard*, another tramp."

"So we're on a whole different ship?" Bert said petulantly.

Ace said, "And the slower of the two. The *Sea Leopard* is faster in the water than the *Diving Loon*."

"So we'll arrive late, too? Phooie."

"You should not pine for the actress so, Bert!" Sam scolded.

"Who says I'm pining?" Bert protested.

"Yew mirror a melancholy mastiff, meladdo!" Gooper nodded his ginger-topped head.

Quack stroked his shaved chin and smirked. "I might see her tomorrow. I get to be Wizenby the tractor man again."

"Oh, you shallow hack!" Bert's mood continued to plummet.

Chapter 10

To look at the *Sea Leopard* was to wince. The ship was tied up at the lowest-rent pier in the city. Shabby masts and peeling deckhouses grew like haphazard warts atop its rust-streaked hull. Gangplanks poked into open cargo bays, each barnlike cavity uglier on the inside than out, if that were possible. An extra boiler and smokestack were awkwardly grafted on at the stern for extra speed.

The crowded dock hummed with activity. The tide would turn in an hour, and several ships intended to sail when it did, including the *Sea Leopard*.

Captain Landstrad was no joy to look at, either. He wore a perpetual frown under his shock of gray hair, and every word that struggled free of his dour mouth emerged world-weary and cynical.

"Awlreet!" he bawled at Wizenby the tractor sales-man. "Awlreet, *now* ye can drive yer tractor up the gangplank. Yer tractor is first off, see? All them crates stay aboard until after all that. First in, last off. Ele-mentary, reet?"

"Finally!" gruffed Wizenby, then amended, "I mean, yes, sir! Thank you, sir!"

Wizenby fired up the bulldozer and engaged its low gear. A scrawny sailor backed up the gangplank in Wizenby's sight. The young sailor waved his hands as if his motions were guiding the tractor up the ramp and into the cargo hold. Wizenby ignored the youth and crawled the dozer up and in. He parked the brand-new diesel tractor in front of the crates, as the captain had ordered. He dismounted and wheezed at the gawky young sailor, "Receipt, if you please."

As Wizenby waited for his receipt, another truck arrived. Three scruffy figures swaggered out, one man and two women. The truck bed held crates marked "Ammunition" and "Explosives." The three swaggerers brayed loudly for assistance.

Wizenby muttered under his breath, "Hired guns." But he couldn't watch long. His receipt in hand, he trudged to the Acme Heavy Industries truck parked dockside.

Gooper bulked behind the driver's wheel, cap pulled low over his eyes. He fired up the engine, clashed the gears, and rolled off Pier 71, around the block, and out of sight. And that was journey's end. He parked.

As the truck engine rattled to a stop, Gooper eyed Quack. "Any new clues, mate?"

"Three mercenaries and some crates full of ordnance. Miss Murchison expects trouble. Big trouble."

Ace, Bert, Sam, and Tombstone were all lined up on top of a closed garbage dumpster. They shared two pairs of binoculars between them, peering out over a wall at the end of the alley, overlooking the pier. Gooper and Quack joined the row of spies.

Bert welcomed Quack back with a sneer. "You missed seeing her, Machiavelli!"

"'Were I like thee I'd throw away myself!'" orated Quack.

"That was from Shakespeare," Sam commented with a little smile. He stroked the curled ends of his black mustache.

Ace scanned the bustling dockside through binoculars. Gooper pulled a rat out of his pocket by the tail and set it down on the lid of the dumpster.

Tombstone glanced at the rat. "Why th' heck don't it run off now? Git, varmint! Be free!"

Gooper's mustache drooped. "'E likes me."

Tombstone eyed Gooper up and down. "Ah don't. Tastes differ, Ah reckon."

"I am worried," Ace said, lowering the binoculars. She frowned at the *Sea Leopard*.

"Worried we're goin' t' miss departin' on our own ship?" Tombstone wondered.

"Worried for Miss Murchison. I see her taxi now. The port authority told me her name over the phone, so she didn't bother to disguise her intentions. And now she's about to board in plain sight. She should have been more secretive."

"Y'think Captain Braun's gonna know? And then do somethin'?"

"Exactly so."

She glanced left and right at her five companions in adventure.

Over their faces for a moment, a brief vision of a snow leopard appeared. Ace heard her own voice telling a Nepalese monk of the lesson taught her by the big cat, "I should live to be of help. Help to others, I mean."

Bumbling collections of quirks they might be, but they were also gentlemen of honor, steadfast and true.

A cozy warmth spread over Ace, but her keen eyes speared toward the dock. Under a floppy hat, Marilyn Murchison wore sunglasses that would fool no one. Even before she paid the cabby, most of the crew of the *Sea Leopard* clustered around her like flies on syrup.

Abruptly, Ace was all business. "Change of plan. You five go. Catch the *Diving Loon* at Pier 68. I'll stow away on the *Sea Leopard*. Remember, disembark on the small island that sits west of Sius itself. Unload our equipment. I will meet you there."

Ace was already moving. She hopped lightly down from the dumpster and ran up the alleyway, swift and silent. In moments, she was gone from sight.

Ace's associates all loved action. It was a bitter blow when necessity demanded activities less fraught with danger. "Awww!" moped Gooper, "I want ter stow away!"

"You snore like a buzz saw," Tombstone said.

"So do you, flimsy stick man!"

"Walrus!"

"Toothpick!"

Bert said wearily, "Oh, shut up, you two. Let's go catch our ship."

Ace dangled $10 in front of a Pier 71 clothing wholesaler. The merchant said, "The whole rack? Well. All right."

"I need the rack itself, too. Is that a problem?"

The aproned merchant gazed raptly into the golden eyes and said faintly, "No. No, that won't be a problem, ma'am. Thank you for your custom."

Ace winked and wheeled the rack away. She buried her upper body among the frocks on the rack as she passed Miss Murchison's taxi and rolled up the *Sea Leopard*'s gangplank. She walked almost blind and had to trust her instinct. But her luck held. The crew of the *Sea Leopard* had eyes only for Miss Murchison and paid no attention to the self-driving rack of dresses. The clothes rack worked its way belowdecks. Soon, Ace was alone down in the cargo hold among piles of boxes and crates.

"Easy as stone soup, if I do say so myself," Ace mused as she shifted a few crates to make a hidey-hole. "But if it was easy for me, it would be easy for anybody."

The tide turned. A harbor pilot boarded. The crew cast off the lines. An hour later, the *Sea Leopard* cleared the harbor. The pilot clambered off. The engines throbbed to a full, deep rumble, and they steamed off across the Atlantic Ocean.

Chapter II

After a catnap, Ace exercised. Ace's daily rituals began when she was a child and grew ever more rigorous as she matured. Ace mastered the merely difficult and soared on to physical feats that bordered upon impossible. The routines started with recognizable calisthenics then moved on to gymnastics. Then she meditated, tensing and relaxing each individual muscle in her body. Simultaneously, Ace mentally counted back in time to visualize ancient calendar pages. Her skin shone with perspiration as she encompassed dual mental and physical challenges. Her senses were the last things she tuned up. She used autohypnosis to make her irises expand and contract. Concentrated attention stretched the dynamic range of her hearing. Meditating on her sense of touch allowed her to feel air currents and the fleeting touches of individual threads of fabric. Had she been back in the lab at Wall Street and Broadway, she would have uncorked a rack of jars containing various scents to sharpen her sense of smell. She would have sampled various chemicals and minerals to improve the powers of discernment in her sense of taste.

As the steamer churned its way across the Atlantic, Ace nested atop piled shipping crates. She used her copious free time well. Hours sped by in simple appreciation of the beauty of ocean and sky. She also mentally outlined a technical article on soft tissue surgery and composed a piano duet. She sketched and rejected several airship designs.

When night blanketed the world, she roamed about the ship, moving like a golden ghost. She stayed out of view of the pilot in the wheelhouse, of course, but she explored everywhere else with ease.

The crew of four consisted of old, gruff Captain Landstrad; a young and scrawny lad named Harpstone who pulled all the night watches; Lucky, an even scrawnier but much older sailor who could still shimmy up the mainmast at the drop of a hat; and Turnbull, a robust bewhiskered engine expert. The big ship could use double that number of crewmen, but Landstrad was a tightwad.

Miss Murchison and her trio of hirelings occupied passenger cabins. Ace wanted to call them Rock, Paper, and Scissors, but their real names were Garbruck, Stennis, and Clout. Each was more intimidating than the last. Garbruck, the only male, bald, thick, solid, and bowlegged. Stennis, blonde, one-eyed, and tall as a Valkyrie. Clout, broad, quick, short black hair, a lacework of scars across her face. Four times a minute, Clout spat contemptuously off to one side.

Marilyn Murchison referred to them as her crew of excavators, but they strutted around encrusted with knives and guns. They made a point of lounging with exaggerated laziness every time a regular crew member worked nearby.

On the first night at sea, Ace spotted the forward navigation lights of a vessel on the horizon, following them. The luminous dots grew neither closer nor further away as the night wore on. The next night, they were still there. The *Sea Leopard* sailed in a shipping lane, and other ships passed daily. Still, the likelihood of a following ship to have exactly the same speed and course loomed ominously low in Ace's calculations.

Once in a while during her nighttime prowls, Ace experienced a prickly certainty of some other presence nearby. She could never pinpoint anything concrete, but her conviction grew that eyes other than hers watched from the shadows.

In the deep of night, when only the helmsman stood awake by the wheel and compass, Ace checked for traces of other passengers. All the cabins that ought to be empty lay clean and bare. She ran into no strangers above decks or below.

On the third day, Clout and Garbruck played a game on the stern. One threw empty bottles into the air, and the other shot them to fragments before they splashed down in the waves. The har-hars and gunfire grated on Ace's nerves so much she had to calm herself with Wing Chun meditation.

On the third night, Ace thought she saw a child climbing in the rigging. In the moonless gloom, the outlines blurred, but Ace gained the impression of a small body nimbly climbing aloft. The next minute, it was gone. Ace investigated but found nothing except an orange peel on the deck.

On the fourth night, Ace made free with the ship's washroom to launder her flight suit. After, she sauntered around the lonely deck.

A blotch on the deck caught her eye. She knelt to find a smeared blob of guano. Copious quantities of bird poo was a nautical inevitability, but this guano was fresh. Ace wished for some laboratory gear, but of course, none was available. The statistic of significance in Ace's mind was the number of seagulls about the *Sea Leopard*. There were none. Clout and Garbruck had frightened off the few remaining seabirds on the previous day, and they had not returned.

With the back of her neck prickling with the certainty that she was being watched, Ace crept back to her hiding place in the cargo hold.

On the fifth night, Stennis died.

CHAPTER 12

On the fifth night, the winds kicked up. The seas rose. The ship rode swells heavier than any so far. The distance between wave crests grew longer than the ship itself. Ace exercised and meditated in the cargo hold as the ship reeled drunkenly. The ship fell forward into each wave trough and then smacked into the next watery hill with a thudding concussion. After the bow split the next wave into foamy halves, the ship tilted and climbed, only to arc over with a metallic groan and repeat the process. Idly, she timed the period between shuddering booms.

After meditation, she ascended all the way to the *Sea Leopard*'s rusty mast and crow's nest. On previous nights, Ace had tracked the distant following ship from this vantage. Tonight, the gigantic rolling swells waved the crow's nest like a flag on a stick and invited nausea.

Ace glanced down at the deck. A person-sized shadow moved along the rail. The form caught brief illumination as it passed the porthole of a lit cabin. It was Stennis. The blonde mercenary managed to retain her swagger even in the heavy seas.

Ace watched the shadowy deck walker for a minute then returned to ship-spotting. Only when the *Sea Leopard* crested the top of a wave could she scan the aft horizon.

A faint, irritated "Hey!" reached Ace's ears from below. It sounded like Stennis's voice. Far below,

Stennis was a vague, dark blob on the deck that moved and changed shape.

Stennis snarled, quietly and distinctly, "You!"

A metallic flash of reflected light gleamed for a moment. The blob of shadow moved jerkily, and Ace heard grunts.

And then the scream rang out, ripped from nightmare fabric, horror-stricken and jarring. Ace stood up in alarm.

On the heels of the scream, a growl rasped the air. The unearthly growl instantly brought a cold sweat and raised the hackles. It emanated from the shadowy scene on the deck and permeated the ship with its eerie, menacing ululation.

Ace swarmed down the mast, feet and hands frantically searching for holds in the wet netting of the rope ladder. It seemed a long, long journey.

As she landed on the deck, the crew boiled up from below. Ace scuttled forward and kept moving to avoid discovery as the crew swept the deck with electric torches.

"What was that?" scrawny young Harpstone wondered.

"Nevah heard the like befoah!" old Lucky wheezed.

The crew pounded around, waving their electric torches. After circumnavigating the deck, the crew congregated back at the hatch.

"Nothin,'" reported Turnbull.

"Nothin' here, either," Harpstone contributed.

"Nothin' to be seen. Maybe it was an albatross havin' some kinda spasm," Lucky griped.

"Screaming. Growling. Gah! Gives me the shivers!" Harpstone said, with feeling.

They filed back down belowdecks, still muttering conversation. Ace seized the moment and padded to where she had seen the shadowy movements. Scanning to the limits of her vision, she saw no people.

Hunkering down, though, Ace spotted a dark stain on the deck. She touched it.

Slightly warm and very wet.

She sniffed it.

The coppery smell of fresh blood.

She examined the railing, beyond which the dark sea foamed and heaved. More spots of blood glistened on the rail. Had there been someone near to Ace, they would have heard a new sound. A contralto humming that seemed to emanate from the very air itself, vibrant and somehow beautiful and eerie at the same time.

Then Ace heard the crew's voices getting louder. Footsteps, also. She whisked away again, into the companionway.

"Stennis!" came a querying shout.

"Stennis, where are you? Stennis!"

But there was no answer. There would never be an answer.

CHAPTER 13

Turnbull the engineer's heavy tread vibrated the deck. Ace whisked into the dark of the nearest companionway. She hugged the rusty wall as Turnbull clomped past. The beam of his electric torch made the air fill with thousands of streaking dots of sea spray. The pitching deck tangled the feet, and the rushing wind confused the ear.

The engines and wind noise masked new footsteps. A short person brushed by her in the companionway, trailing a wake of body odor and rum.

Ace blinked, but there was no sign that she had been detected. Her nose wrinkled in disgust, but the storm soon cleared the earthy funk. Ace's brow furrowed. No one on board was that short, not even scrawny Harpstone or demure Marilyn Murchison.

Ace crouched low and scuttled crabwise after the smelly apparition into the spray-laced wind. A feral smile crept onto her face. Someone to hunt. A bit of good luck, at last.

The smelly skulker headed forward. Ace followed. She could see his shadowy outline until he rounded a deck housing. He did not reappear. Ace froze, feeling exposed on deck. Furthermore, Ace heard Turnbull clomping from aft. She whipped her head around to see him swinging his electric torch back and forth, approaching steadily.

Ace grimaced and darted her eyes up, forward,

back, left, right. No hiding places. Ace sprang to the portside railing and vaulted it. Her feet dangled over the smooth rusty sides of the *Sea Leopard*. Below, the Atlantic Ocean heaved and roiled, mighty and unforgiving.

Ace's arms hugged tight to the railing until Turnbull's light drew too close. With discovery imminent, she ducked and disappeared from view altogether.

"Gotcha!" a reedy tenor whined from toward the bow.

"Uh?" Turnbull shone his light forward.

By luck, Turnbull's action was the smartest possible thing. Blinded by the sudden flash of light, the owner of the reedy voice had poor aim when he opened fire. The distinctive rattle of a tommy gun tore through the squally air. Bullets ricocheted and whined off the rusty steel of the rails and deck housings. Turnbull gave a croaked cry.

All too nearby, Ace was quietly panicking. She never expected a machine gun battle. She clung to the side of the ship with her hands inside a scupper, a drain opening along the otherwise solid deck railing. But her steely fingers already felt the strain. Shrapnel or bullets could end her tenuous hold, and she would drop into the churning Atlantic.

The bullet storm let up momentarily. Then the stream of bullets was answered from aft. Marilyn's man, Garbruck, yelled, "Eat hot lead!" The reedy tenor gunman seemed eager to comply, opening fire, filling the deck with bullets.

Ace took several deep breaths. She transferred all her weight to one hand stuck in the scupper, with two legs braced against the exterior of the ship. Her free hand flew to her wide belt and fished.

Sudden pain lanced through her overstrained, exposed fingers. A wild bullet had carved a furrow through flesh. Her injured hand lost strength. It began to slip as blood made the scupper slippery. Ace danced with death, and she knew it. With only moments before her agonized hand gave way, Ace seized upon the coiled cord she was seeking. It was strong but thin. Desperately, she flung the coil at a block and tackle several yards out of reach.

The wind blew the cord wildly. As Ace's injured hand collapsed, her seeking hand touched the waving end of the cord. Madly, she twisted her hand to wrap the cord and secure herself as she fell toward the ocean. A rising Atlantic swell swatted her like a gnat and battered her body against the rusty side of the *Sea Leopard*. Ace fought to hold on, fought for consciousness, fought against a cold resting place on the sea floor.

Back on deck, Garbruck screamed in pain. The hail of bullets ceased.

The reedy tenor said, "Hah. I know that voice. It sounded like that loser, Garbruck. I hate that guy."

The short man eased out from behind his sheltering deckhouse and peered aft. "Well, he's out of commission. Let's see who else on this ship wants to go head to head wit' da mighty Mutt-man. Damn that Braun for keepin' me holed up fer days. See how easy this is?" He emitted a nasty tenor laugh.

The gunman's laugh cut off. Two booted feet crashed into the back of his head. "Ow!" A dripping wet, flight-suited figure landed on top of him. "Uff!" A sinewy hand wrenched his hot-barreled machine gun from his jellied grasp. "Hey!" And then the hot cylinder of metal crashed down on his skull.

He slumped and protested no more.

Ace breathed hard and tossed the tommy gun overboard. She bent to examine the rat-like, pinch-faced little man. "Mutt-man? Seriously? That's your nick?"

As blood dripped steadily from Ace's fingertips, she talked herself through the situation. "One well-armed goon. Can't assume there aren't more. Mutt-man mentioned Braun, so he's definitely aboard."

Ace's jaw clenched. "Marilyn!"

Ace raced aft.

She passed a capstan, behind which a prone shadow groaned. She passed a companionway, spotting another body-like shape crumpled inside. She stepped over the hummock she presumed was Garbruck's body and dived down the stairs. This passage led past the larger cabins toward the engine room.

The hallway was dimly lit. As Ace skittered down, she saw a vague flicker of movement at the very end of the hall. She passed the captain's cabin. Marilyn Murchison's was next, but the door was open, and there was no one inside. Ace opened all the cabin doors as she passed. No one.

Ducking inside the last cabin, Ace stole a sock and knotted it around her lacerated fingers using her other hand and her teeth. "Clean, thank goodness," she muttered.

The hall ended with stairs down to the engine room. Ace tried to get her head as low as possible, crouching as she minced down the metal stairs. The upper level of the engine room came into view, really just a grid of catwalks around the boilers. Two inadequate bare electric light bulbs and the angry red glow of the furnaces below cast murky, wavering illumination.

Ace's jaw clenched. An easy stone's throw away on the iron mesh of the catwalk, the hunched form of a man crouched atop the prone body of a slender woman. He worked with his hands, his back to Ace. The woman's legs kicked feebly. She was alive.

Ace accelerated down the stairs. Her boots clattered.

The heavy man whipped around to glare at Ace. Deep-set, shadowed eyes darkened a gray-whiskered face. Ace reached the catwalks, but the man spun and rose, lifting the woman as if she weighed nothing. Handling Marilyn Murchison with brusque power, he choked her in the crook of one arm. The other hand snapped up with a metallic flash. He held the knife to Murchison's pale throat.

"Hold it right there!" His gruff accented voice, bushy sideburns tinged with gray, and a shabby naval coat with three bars on the sleeve left no doubt; this was Bengt Braun.

Ace's keen eyes studied the carbon steel knife. Its edge pressed cruelly against Marilyn's skin. Where blade met hilt, there was a dark rust-red smear. A chill prickled her skin. That smear was blood.

Stennis's blood. The murderer had yet to fully clean his instrument of death.

Chapter 14

Bengt Braun demanded, "Who're you?"

"Call me Ace. Bengt Braun, I presume." Ace hovered about a dozen feet from captive and captor and spoke with a measured cadence. Marilyn was gagged, but Ace's arrival had interrupted the binding of her hands. Marilyn stared. A glint of hope sparked deep in her fear-glazed eyes.

"Ace? Ace Carroway?" A greedy grin sharpened the sea captain's blunt face, revealing a tobacco-stained gap between his lower teeth. "Well, Ace Carroway, if you don't do as I say, I slit her throat." He shook Marilyn effortlessly.

"Calm. There is no need for threats. I am not armed." Ace was coiled up tighter than a watch spring, but she schooled her voice to be low and smooth.

"Turn around. Put your hands behind your back."

Ace considered the order. Her eyes flicked from where steel dimpled Marilyn's neck to Braun's avid, hungry smile. Every animal instinct in her protested, but slowly, she rotated. He and his bloody knife swam from her field of view.

"Don't worry, I won't kill you. There's a bounty on your head." Gleeful greed colored Braun's words.

"I know," Ace said through clenched teeth[4]. "Plan-

---

[4] It was a black-market bounty, offered by Ace's Great War adversary Darko Dor.

ning on collecting it, huh?"

"It's my lucky day," Braun agreed. He muttered to Marilyn Murchison, "You're lucky, too, dollface. I'm a generous man, not to kill you straightaway."

"You hired Mutt-man?" Ace asked. She held her hands behind her, as requested. She also widened her stance and bent slightly at the knees. This shifted her weight to the balls of her feet, a pose readied for action.

"Mutt Maloney? The little rat's been itching to shoot everybody. I finally let him." Braun chuckled. He grunted for a few moments then told Marilyn, "There, you're a neat package now, all tied up in string."

"Human lives mean nothing to you," Ace said bitterly.

"Shut your mouth. Come here."

He grabbed Ace's hands.

The touch was what Ace was waiting for. The logic was simple. If Braun had hands to tie her up, he had no hands for knives.

She dropped into a crouch, breaking his grip. Launching into the air, she spun. She extended a leg. In a roundhouse kick, her boot struck Braun on the side of the head.

With a pained grunt, he tottered to one side, flailing. He reached for his knife, sheathed at his hip.

Ace touched down briefly, only to spring in the air again. This time, she grabbed for a ceiling pipe valve wheel. With two feet this time, she smashed Braun's shoulder in a piledriver kick.

Checked at the hip, the heavy pirate spun over the railing. His knife arm arced, slashing even as he fell.

Ace felt a pluck as her flight suit was opened at the thigh. A bright burn of pain scored along her leg.

Ace landed in a crouch. Bengt Braun's heavy body bounced off a boiler then slithered to the floor of the lower level, out of sight. He did not cry out. Dead thuds sounded as his soft, heavy body hit metal surfaces. His murderous knife jolted free and clattered down to the lower level.

Ace's gaze flicked to Marilyn Murchison. The actress stared at Ace over her gag. Her hands were bound behind her, and she weaved on her feet as the ship rolled.

"Surprise," Ace said with a lopsided smile. "Really, Marilyn. We have to stop meeting like this."

When her gag was released, the blonde rubbed her mouth with trembling hands and panted. "Ugh! I hate that man! Ace, come on! Clout went to help Garbruck. There was a gun battle!" Marilyn launched herself forward toward the hall of cabins.

Ace followed, feeling a sluice of blood flow warmly down her leg. Gray motion caught her eye. She paused to watch a small shape descend downward from the ceiling and disappear behind a boiler, indistinct in the gloom. Its motion was almost spiderlike as it descended.

Ace was slow to follow Marilyn as the actress clattered up the engine room stairs. She had a strong impulse to chase the ghostly climber and make sure Braun was neutralized. But warm blood sluiced down her leg. Ace limped forward. "Marilyn, where is the nearest first aid kit?"

Marilyn glanced back at the limping flyer. "Oh, Ace! How could I not see? You are injured. Come on. The captain's cabin has bandages. Are you all right? Oh dear, I feel such the heel. You saved my life again, and here I am all in a tizzy."

As they reached the captain's cabin, there was a clatter of many feet on the stairs down from the deck. Captain Landstrad clomped down first. Scrawny Harpstone escorted Turnbull, who held a bloody left arm against his body. Next came old Lucky, who steadied Garbruck, whose face was streaked by rivulets of bright blood streaming down over one eye. Clout came last, dragging the unconscious body of Mutt Maloney by the collar.

Captain Landstrad glowered at Ace. "Who in blazes are you?"

A babble erupted. Despite the din, names were exchanged and the roll of bandages was passed around.

"I met Mutt Maloney a time or two," Garbruck offered up. "Nasty. Pure nasty."

"'Nasty,' says Garbruck! Ha!" Clout laughed nasally and spat to one side.

Ace ripped her flight suit slash open wider and wrapped gauze around her thigh laceration. She said, "Captain, please send Clout, Harpstone, and Lucky to collect Bengt Braun from the engine room. I don't know how badly he's hurt, and we don't want him running loose."

Marilyn nodded. "Yes! Yes, please!"

But when Clout and crew arrived, the engine room was unoccupied.

♣ ♣ ♣

The weather calmed the next day. Harpstone was set to swab blood from the deck. Blood from Stennis, Turnbull, and Garbruck. Stennis's was the only death. Turnbull escaped with a hole through his arm. Garbruck had a peppering of splinters and flak plus a bullet graze to his bald temple. (Over the next few days, he refused to change his blood-splotched head bandage and walked with extra swagger.) They locked Mutt Maloney in a bare cabin.

Stowaway secret blown, Ace moved into a cabin. She slept and showered. With her injured fingers and slashed thigh rebandaged, she sought Marilyn Murchison. Under Clout's suspicious eye, they strolled the deck.

"What is this all about, Marilyn?" Ace asked. "What are you and Braun chasing?"

Marilyn gazed to the horizon unseeingly. "Soon," she said. "I'll tell you soon."

"That's all I get? Just a brush-off?" Ace's mouth compressed to a hard line.

"I'm sorry, Ace, but it's for the best. It really is." The actress turned to Ace with a face set in stone, chin lifted and jaw set.

"For the record, I beg to differ." Ace arched an eyebrow at Marilyn. The hard stare lasted a moment longer, then a pair of wry smiles followed. A truce had been declared, at least for the moment.

Marilyn's voice softened. "Thank you again for looking after me. I'd be lost without you. How did you know about the *Sea Leopard*? How did *he* know about the *Sea Leopard*?"

Ace ticked points off on her fingers. "You hired the

boat, the crew, mercenaries, a taxi cab, and supplies, including a bulldozer, all in the open. Furthermore, unlike us detectives, Braun knew you were heading to Sius."

Marilyn's eyes dropped to her feet. "Oh."

"Don't feel bad. What it means is that you're not used to undercover work."

"That's true enough." The actress tucked a stray lock of blonde hair behind her ear.

Ace said, "I have a riddle for you. What is gray, about the size of a breadbox, and likes to climb or crawl?"

The blonde scrunched up her nose. "What?"

"No, seriously, I've caught two glimpses of something small and nimble."

"Oh! Well, that's probably just Braun's pet monkey."

Ace went slightly popeyed. She admitted, "That would explain it!"

♠ ♠ ♠

Despite another search by all the crew, neither Braun nor his hiding place was discovered.

That night, a lifeboat vanished. The theft was stealthy. Not even Ace heard the winches unwinding. The haunting feeling of being watched evaporated.

There was a general feeling of relief mixed with an uneasy feeling of ominous dread. Mutt Maloney was still safely, though seldom quietly, locked in a cabin.

In the day, the *Sea Leopard* passed the Straits of

Gibraltar and into the Mediterranean Sea. The wind and waters calmed. A bright, sparkling sun shone over the warm seas.

Belatedly, Clout and Garbruck discovered a storage locker by the engine room with evidence of recent occupation.

The Murchison expedition gathered to talk it over. Clout crowed, "Found a lot of food trash and Mutt Maloney's kit. Braun got scared off the ship, I bet." She spit off to one side.

"All right. Fair enough," Marilyn Murchison said. "But he's still alive and breathing down our necks, and he knows we're going to Sius. Who knows where he is or what he is up to."

Ace spotted no distant running lights that night. Next day, beyond the eastern horizon, a gargantuan blood-tipped triangle hove into view. It was the island of Sius. They had arrived.

CHAPTER 15

Ace stuck her head out a porthole to watch the approach. From a distance, the legendary isle of Sius resembled a lumpy cone. Crimson mineral deposits splattered the flat top of the cone and trailed down the slopes like rivulets of blood on a grand scale. Tales of the "blood bath of the gods" had chilled wide-eyed listeners for untold generations. Ace admitted to herself, "It does look gory!"

Mt. Sisuvius was the name of Sius's volcano, one of the most active known. Steam plumes and ash clouds ceaselessly billowed up from its cratered peak. It last erupted some years before the outbreak of the Great War.

Closer up, the terrain resolved into jumbled lava flows that poked out into the calm sea like gnarled starfish arms. Sheltered between the lava arms lay valleys full of lush green trees, thinner than a jungle but thicker than a savannah.

The *Sea Leopard* passed south of Sius. Ace spotted the small western isle where she had told her associates to land. The tiny lump was a rocky hazard to ships but little more. In the main island valleys, she caught a glimpse of a flowing herd of antelope. Her sharp eyes picked out three giraffe heads and necks poking up out of the scrub.

The ship arced north, heading for the easternmost edge where a partial harbor was evident. Ace shucked her boots off and tied them to her belt.

"Time to go explore," Ace said cheerfully.

Casually, she jackknifed out the porthole and bounced off the deck and over the rail into a swan dive. The sea swallowed her with barely a gulp.

Sans Ace, the *Sea Leopard* sidled up alongside a spur of congealed lava jutting out into the Mediterranean. The crew lashed the *Sea Leopard* to the primitive dock and began unloading. Unloading the bulldozer in particular.

Meanwhile, Ace swam to shore. She slipped out of the calm water between black lava spokes onto a tiny beach. Ace peeled off her sopping flight suit and wrung it dry. Damp but tolerably comfortable, she hiked into the forest, heading toward the *Sea Leopard*'s eastern mooring.

Ace crossed the jumbled terrain with difficulty. Harsh, jagged lava outcrops loomed unexpectedly. The twisted blobs of rock seemed always to block the desired direction of travel. Furthermore, the spaces between were often filled with the boles of trees. Ace moved catlike around and over the obstacles.

She paused to breathe the fresh air, inhaling deep. Her hand rested on a lava boulder as she listened to the rustle of leaves and the calls of birds. Nearby, a southern boubou called. For a moment, the birdsong transported Ace to South Africa.

Ace yelped. A sharp pain lanced on the webbing

between her forefinger and thumb. She slapped at the spot then plucked a biting ant off. The tiny body gleamed dark red and felt as hard as a bead. She shuddered in recognition. A siafu ant.

Hastily, she examined her boots and legs, but no blanket of ants swarmed there. She told the ant pinched in her left hand, "You're the last thing I wanted to meet here. Between you and a murderous sea captain, I'd prefer the crazy captain."

As she clambered off the lava arm to a flatter, more overgrown area, a gravel ribbon met her eyes. What had once been a road had become overgrown with plants and a few saplings, but it had been clear and level in the past. It stretched east toward the ship's berth in one direction and toward the volcano in the other. Ace hiked inland, following the road. It was a short journey. The road ended at the root of Mt. Sisuvius where a tunnel bored into the cliff face. Originally, the tunnel was a lava tube, a natural volcanic channel.

But human hands had shaped it somewhat. Metal gates lay in twisted ruin off to one side. A jumble of animal cages large and small were piled in the same dump area along with the rusting skeleton of a Great War-era flatbed truck.

Ace padded into the tunnel, eyes roving, mind spinning. After forty yards, blocks of rock fallen from the ceiling barred any further progress.

"Clearing these stones is an excellent use for a clawed bulldozer," Ace murmured. She clambered around, inspecting in the dim light. "But even with the tractor, it will take days."

The stone walls quivered with an abrupt rumble. A

low grinding sound rolled back and forth in the tunnel, and the ground shook. Dust drizzled down from the ceiling.

The volcano was restless.

♠♠♠

Ace quit the tunnel and climbed the spur, with the idea to find an observation post. The knife slash on her leg ached but did not slow her. She shimmied up a tree in time to watch the Allis-Chalmers bulldozer crawl out of the *Sea Leopard* and onto shore. But the sun was westering. The cool of evening already caressed the skin.

According to her research, years ago the island had served as a sort of game preserve for Ottoman hunters. There could be lions. Perhaps even elephants. Ace meandered upslope, eyes and ears alert.

She discovered vines of wild grapes and paused for a snack. As she munched on sweet orbs, quiet rustlings pricked her ears. She held still, and her eyes widened in wonder. Small bodies weaved through the scrub. A foraging herd of dik-diks, small antelope with large eyes, tiny, single horns, and elongated snouts surrounded her. The tallest of them barely reached her knee.

When night fell, Ace curled up in a person-sized bubble cave formed ages ago by gases expanding in congealing lava. In the quiet and dark of the night, she slept.

Volcano rumbles woke her. Morning light streamed into her little cave. She stretched and yawned and gazed upward at the bloody crown of Mt. Sisuvius. The volcano belched a plume of ash-laden steam. Today's volcanic venting dwarfed yesterday's, and the billowing gray-black cloud blotted out much of the sky.

After her exercises, Ace descended, feeding on olives and more grapes. At the tunnel entrance, engine noise echoed inside the lava tube. A lazy shimmer of bluish smoke hung around the tunnel's mouth.

Ace spotted a wide-brimmed, floppy hat amongst the nearby trees. Marilyn Murchison took her ease on a log, watching and listening to the work going on in the smoky, dusty lava tube. Aside from the boutique-bought hat she wore more practical safari khakis.

Ace crept near, using the trees as cover. Clout and Garbruck used the claw dozer and chains to drag boulders, one by one, out of the tunnel. It was a slow, laborious process. Ace waited until the mercenaries were inside the tunnel, then she tossed a stick. It chuffed into the grass next to the actress. Marilyn turned around with a fearful glance, but there was only a quiet, golden-skinned woman waving hello.

"Ace!" she exclaimed, leaping to her feet. "Ace Carroway, by heavens, you gave me a start!" Marilyn fanned herself.

"Hello, Marilyn," Ace said, staying in the shadow of a tree.

"I wondered where you'd gone. We couldn't find you when we were unloading or in the night." The blonde moved toward Ace a few paces, wringing her hands.

"I was scouting. Were you aware this island has siafu ants?"

"Siafu? Oh, those nasty red ants?" Marilyn wrinkled up her nose. "I'm aware."

"They're dangerous, if you're anywhere near a colony."

Marilyn nodded vigorously. "Yes! I've seen a man who was bitten. It was hideous."

"The last time you visited Sius, you mean."

Marilyn's face colored. She replied hotly, "Ace Carroway, you're too smart for your own good!"

"You haven't told me the *why* of all this, Marilyn. What's in the tunnel that you and Braun want so much?"

Murchison glanced back at the noisy, dusty tunnel, then at Ace, then down at her feet. "Don't ask that, Ace. Please?" Marilyn spread her hands in entreaty. "I know I didn't tell you everything back in New York, but I told you as much as I could. I know I might be doing the wrong thing, and I know I might be the world's biggest fool. But I'm still betting that all this works out for me. And I can't tell you what. I *can't.*"

Ace gazed at her until the actress squirmed. But a defiant light ignited in Marilyn's eye. She straightened up and jutted out her lower jaw.

Ace smiled faintly. "All right, if that's how you feel. But I won't be watching over you for a while. I have an errand. Farewell for now, Miss Murchison."

"Farewell? But—"

A gusty roar from the tunnel announced the return of the bulldozer, and Marilyn glanced at the mechanical intruder. When she sought out Ace again, she saw only trees and a slow drizzle of fresh volcanic ash.

CHAPTER 16

Ace's next goal was the western island on the opposite shore of Sius to rendezvous with her associates. She decided to try the northern side of the island rather than the southern. It was a good choice. The north sloped less and was smoother than the south side she had examined from the *Sea Leopard*. The rumblings of blood-topped Mt. Sisuvius continued. Belches of ash from its top grew more frequent.

Ace startled a small herd of impala as she clambered over a jagged spur of lava. She paused to admire the athletic grace of their departure. Upon spotting a siafu ant mound, Ace detoured around it widely. She also jogged past a placidly grazing giraffe, but she didn't see any evidence of rhinoceros or elephant.

Descending into the next valley, Ace smelled woodsmoke. The homey scent contrasted with the acrid, sulfuric smells that wafted from Mt. Sisuvius.

Ace slowed to cast about for the source. From altogether too near for comfort intruded a snarl, tuba deep and feral. The powerful rattle vibrated the spine and galvanized buried, instinctive impulses to run. Ace froze, eyes wide, heart racing.

She reached to her wide belt, but the most weapon-like object there was a screwdriver.

She palmed its inadequateness anyway and stalked forward toward the snarl sound. She heard it again, the animal sound seemingly inches away.

A human voice stuttered in formal Greek, "Oh,

goddess of wisdom, save this mortal from the doom that awaits, I pray! Your servant ever I shall be, humble and true!"

Ace passed a pair of trees and saw them.

The lion paced back and forth below a small, slender tree. Lean and tawny, its mighty jaws hung open in a hungry "C" shape. A thick-maned male, it outweighed Ace three to one.

The small tree bent under the weight of a young man. Curly black hair topped simple homespun trousers and a loose-fitting, white shirt. He clung to the tree, tracking the motions of the lion with fear-widened eyes as he prayed. The faint copper tang of blood scented the air. A trickle of red ran down the smooth, white-gray bark of the poplar.

In the next heartbeat, the lion leaped. Its claws raked upward. The man moved his lower leg just in time. The claws sliced across the slender trunk, ripping through the bark as if it were mere fluff.

Ace inhaled.

The whisper of sound was tiny, but the lion whipped its head around and faced her. Ace felt the intense focus of its wild gaze like a physical impact. The focused stare promised death. Ace sank lower in her crouch and shuffled back half a pace. She tossed her screwdriver from right hand to left hand. She hooked her free hand partway around the bole of the tree she had passed a moment before. The lion tracked the movement and charged, accelerating like a silent rocket.

Ace stayed still, teeth gritted, muscles coiled. The lion's gallop vibrated through the soles of her feet.

The lion leaped. Ace's right arm pulled, her left leg

pushed, and Ace whisked behind the tree in an eye-blink. The lion twisted in the air. Its killing leap carried it into the tree, and it clipped its shoulder heavily. It ricocheted off the tree and tumbled to the ground, off its feet.

Ace dived on top of the lion. She stabbed the screwdriver into its thick fur and clawed her free hand into the thick mane. The lion twisted and gained its feet as Ace pulled at the mane, scooting her body forward. For a split second, Ace's body sprawled on top of the mass of carnivorous muscle.

The lion shrugged and bucked, twisting. Ace's left hand arced with the screwdriver toward the head of the big cat. The lion roared as Ace's little stab connected.

Shrugging again, the lion threw Ace from its shoulders. Its casual power catapulted her through the air, limbs windmilling. She landed on jagged rocks. The bruising impacts rolled her over, and she landed on her back with a gush of exhaled breath. Desperate for air, Ace found no purchase for her feet as the lion padded toward her. Ace rolled, but the lion batted a paw, reversing the direction of her roll with its effortless power. There was the sound of ripping fabric. Claws of pain raked her ribs.

The lion straddled her body with its front paws and stared down. Ace could feel the moist heat of its breath on her face as the tawny eyes regarded her without pity.

Though Ace's life belonged to the lion, it did not press its advantage. Lethargic, it folded its hind legs, then its front, and collapsed on Ace, pinning her to the ground. Its bright, wild eyes dulled, and it became utterly still. Ace's heart hammered as the lion's lungs emptied, bathing her face in warmth, never to fill again.

CHAPTER 17

Ace struggled for breath. She squirmed, freeing herself from the crush of the lion's body by an inch. "Ow! Oh. Cracked rib? Augh," she wheezed. She wormed out from under the dead lion by painful degrees and dragged herself upright, using the lion's body for support. At last, she straightened up to full height. She gazed down at herself. All there.

She regarded the silent lion ruefully, holding a hand to her ribcage. She scolded it between pained wheezes. "Did I look like food? You must've been awful hungry."

A line appeared between her brows. Her eyes darted about the lion's body, noting its dull coat, distended abdomen, and prominent ribs. "Symptoms of tapeworm. Poor fella. You really *were* hungry."

Her eyes caught motion. The bleeding young man limped with difficulty toward her, brown eyes wide and worshipful. He was of medium height, with broad shoulders. He spoke in formal Greek. "Athena! At my prayer, you descended from Mount Olympus to deliver me from death!"

Ace breathed better now, though each pump of air made her cracked rib bite her with a jolt of pain. She shook her head at the young man. "Ace, not Athena. Do you speak English? My spoken Greek is terrible."

The fellow nodded. Dragging one leg, he inched closer, gazing across the body of the lion at her. "Ace not Athena. As you say. I am Yanni Bennetto."

"Pleased to meet you, Yanni."

"How did you kill the lion?"

"The lion? I inserted a piercing implement into the aural foramen, attempting to angle it upward about twenty-five degrees to cause a brain lesion."

Yanni stared, his jaw going slack. Ace rephrased. "I jammed a screwdriver in his ear." She glanced at the lion. "Apparently, I did manage to nick his brain, for which I am everlastingly grateful. Grateful for screwdrivers, and anatomy class, too."

Yanni's wide eyes expanded even more. He glanced at the lion. A lump of resin sat just behind the jaw and below the external ear. He turned his wonder-filled face to Ace. "My savior. My life is yours, from this day forward."

"Erm."

Yanni held out a hand. "Come. We both bleed. My home is near. There are bandages, there."

"If it really is near, then yes, let's go." Ace also glanced at the nub end of her screwdriver behind the lion's jaw. She decided she didn't want her screwdriver anymore.

She took Yanni's hand and draped his arm over her back. Leaning on her for support, Yanni limped ahead.

Only a few hundred yards away, the source of the woodsmoke Ace had smelled just before the lion attack appeared. The cottage lay enfolded by a garden, a sturdy fence, grapevines, and an olive orchard. A middle-aged woman bent over in the garden, digging up carrots. She straightened and waved her carrots at the approaching pair. She hailed them in Greek. "Yanni! Who is this? What has happened? Are you all right?"

"Mother, this is Athena, though she says to call her

Ace. She just now saved my life! Ace, this is Steffi Bennetto, my mother. My father is Giocco Bennetto."

The party moved inside, where Yanni gratefully collapsed on a divan. A middle-aged man whittled wood at the table. The family resemblance was obvious. "Yanni!" cried Giocco in alarm, dropping his work. Rapid chatter in Greek calmed him.

"A pleasure to meet you, Mr. and Mrs. Bennetto," Ace said. Ace knelt in front of Yanni and examined his clawed lower leg.

"It was a lion," Yanni said.

"A lion!" Giocco cried.

"But they know not to come here." Steffi put a hand over her open mouth.

"One came." Yanni shrugged. His eyes roved over Ace's sure hands and golden hair.

Ace was all business. "Hot water and clean cloths, if you please. I'm a doctor. Yanni will be fine, but he needs stitches." From her belt, she extracted a tiny, flat oilskin package. From the pouch, she plucked a curved suture needle and surgical-strength thread. Over the next half hour, Ace cleaned and stitched Yanni's wounds. Ace blocked from her consciousness her own leaking slashes and twinging jabs of pain from her ribs until Yanni was bandaged.

She managed to convince Yanni that she was from America, not Mount Olympus. At least, she hoped she had.

The family gushed in gratitude and burgeoning affection for Ace. Steffi Bennetto shooed the men out so that Ace could undress and bandage herself. The plump woman insisted upon washing and patching Ace's flight suit and underlying union suit where the lion had slashed it. Steffi forced into Ace's hands a one-piece swimming suit and a robe to wear while the repair was underway. Wearing a wry, bemused expression, Ace complied.

Steffi sat Ace down at the tiny cottage table and fed her an impala roast sandwich and some soup. Ace ate while Yanni gazed at her adoringly and Steffi and Giocco chatted in a mix of Greek and English.

"We are leaving Sius," Giocco said. "Sisuvius will erupt soon. It is not safe to stay. But we are afraid to leave, too. We have been here for many years. Greece will surely be much changed, after the war! We won't know anyone anymore."

"How long have you been here?" Ace asked.

"Nineteen years, haha!" Giocco replied.

"Yanni was born here," Steffi confided.

"We were game wardens, at first. The rich men would come to hunt. We would teach them how to shoot, how to stalk. Everything. They were stupid. Sometimes, we had to teach them how to tie their own shoes." Giocco sniffed contemptuously.

"And then the Great War broke out?" guessed Ace.

"No, no, no! All the giraffes and rhinoceroses were killed. There was nothing left to hunt. We thought the lions were all gone, too. The hunting stopped. Eventually, the Ottomans brought a shipment of giraffes, but then the war broke out. Sius was forgotten." Giocco nodded placidly.

"I see. But you knew about the war," Ace mused.

Steffi nodded. "We have a radio! Well, it no longer works, but we listened for news for a long time. We stayed here. We felt safe here."

"I would like to leave here. I would like to see the

world," Yanni said eagerly.

Giocco replied, "You will, boy, you will. We cannot stay when Sisuvius erupts. We have our boat ready. I am glad the lion did not eat you, we will need your strong arms to row if the wind does not fill the sail."

Yanni smiled at his father then asked Ace unabashedly, "Are all Americans as beautiful as you, Ace?"

Giocco said, "You are nineteen and foolish."

"Eat your soup," admonished Steffi. Her smile to Ace flickered with embarrassment. "I suppose he's never seen a young woman before."

Ace felt heat in her face and changed the subject. "What is underground, two ridges east? People want in there, for some reason."

"Some war thing. We don't know," said Giocco. He worked up some spittle, but a sharp look from Steffi stopped him before he spat.

"There are snakes," Yanni said solemnly.

His parents went shifty-eyed and squirmy at Yanni's pronouncement.

"Mm?" said Ace.

Steffi said apologetically, "Well, there *might* be snakes. It seems reasonable to *assume* that snakes would like it. At least, that is what we told Yanni when he wanted to go down the ventilation shafts."

"Ventilation shafts?" A gleam sprang into Ace's golden eyes.

Chapter 18

The massive, pale-skinned Gooper stood at the prow of the *Diving Loon* and watched the smoking volcano grow larger and larger. His red mustache drooped in desolation.

Standing at his elbow, short, round Sam's black mustache quivered with excitement. He chatted nonstop. "Other Mediterranean cultures have stories, too, sahib! In the preclassical mythology of Crete, Niatta the monstrous dragon of dawn is chained inside Mt. Sisuvius. The hungry dragon Niatta eats all the evil words that people speak and grows bigger and more horrid. But every seventh year, the messenger god, Brevio, comes with his bright sword and slashes at the belly of Niatta. Blood gushes out of the volcano, and so do all the evil words. The hurtful words gather in dark clouds and float away, eventually to become terrible deeds done all over the globe. Romantic, is it not, Gooper?"

Gooper grunted and rolled a meaty shoulder, his sad eyes on the smoking volcano.

Sam looked up at the taller man with sympathy. "The journey is almost over, my friend. The ship is simply too small. We were bound to say things that we would later come to regret. I am sure that Tombstone did not mean what he said about pinheads and knuckle-dragging atavisms."

The biologist squinted down and over at Sam. "Naw, naw, it's not Tombstone that's got me blue. Not this time."

Sam smoothed his mustache. "Ah, yes. Pardon, sahib. I leapt to conclusions. It would be the rat pet, of course."

Gooper's mustache drooped. His eyes grew watery. "'E was a good *Rattus*. 'E could've lived a whole year more, maybe."

Sam patted the muscled hummock of Gooper's shoulder. "You could not know that Captain Foglung kept a cat."

"Two cats."

"Yes, sahib, two cats. Your rat Brownie was outnumbered."

Gooper's mustache quivered with emotion. "This sesquipedalian is done talkin'. If that captain gets high an' mighty on me one more time, I'm just goin' ter break 'im in 'alf." Gooper smacked one ham fist into an open palm.

As if to punctuate Gooper's threat, the volcano belched a new cloud of ash. Glowing cinders arced in slow motion from the crater, tracing graceful trails of gray as they fell. A delayed boom vibrated the *Diving Loon*.

"Sink me!" brayed a voice from behind them. It was Captain Foglung, who stared at the volcano. He pointed a finger at Sam and Gooper and brayed, "I am droppin' you lot off. I am then quittin' the vicinity! If I don't see some hustle outta you lads, I'm quittin' the vicinity before you even unload. Got me?"

Sam surreptitiously threw a left hook into Gooper's midsection. As the musclebound biologist choked and wheezed, Sam soothed, "Aye, aye, sir! We shall hustle and unload, as you say, sir!"

The *Diving Loon* parked its rusty hull next to the tiny western islet and let down the gangplank. The five associates energetically wheeled off a three-wheeled oblong of gleaming steel and glass. It was an airship gondola lacking its balloon. It had a propeller at the back, and at least half a dozen could fit inside. After the gleaming machine and four big crates sat on the dirt of the island, the crew retracted the gangplank. Neither associates nor sailors said goodbye. The *Diving Loon* turned tail and steamed away from the belching volcano.

The associates threw canvas over the cache of gear and then dusted the top of the tarp with handfuls of local dirt. Apparently, when it came time for action, the five could work as a seamless team.

They admired their handiwork.

"It is *camouflage*, as they say in France," Sam said.

"With the dirty tarp over it, it all looks like a big boulder," blond Quack said.

"It can't be seen from the main part of Sius, anyway," brunette Bert added.

There was a pause.

"Wot now?" Gooper wondered.

From behind them all came a dry, teasing voice, "You were supposed to rendezvous with Ace. She said she might be late, but she isn't."

They snapped their heads around to behold a dripping Ace knee-deep in the sea. The westering sun backlit her as she waded to shore. She wore a swimsuit and carried a bundle under one arm.

"Ace!" they chorused.

"Good to see you, fellas! Are you ready to move out? Time might be running short, and I don't mean only the volcano." Ace stowed her wet bundle under the tarp with metallic clank sounds. Freed from her burden, the grinning pilot clasped hands with her associates, one by one.

"You know it, Ace!"

"Been waitin' fer some action!"

"Lead on!"

Sam narrowed his eyes. "You are injured, Lady Ace! What is that on your leg?"

Ace glanced down. "With all I've been through, I almost forgot that one! That's a knife slash courtesy of Bengt Braun. He escaped, I'm sorry to say. He's still at large, and we have to get back to the other side of the island before he does."

"You should take it easy, Ace," Quack said.

Ace snorted and speared him with a cool look.

Quack blinked. He grinned. "You're right. What am I saying?"

Bert wondered, "What's the story, Ace? Did you find out what all this is about?"

Ace raised one of her eyebrows. "Well, fellas, you know how I sometimes keep mum until I'm all the way sure?"

Tombstone moaned. "Yer not gonna tell us anything? Ding-nab it."

"Not so fast, Tombstone. In this case, while plenty of details remain unclear, the central motivation is plain. Absolutely certain, thanks to some ventilation shafts only the locals know about."

Bert said, "Wicked good. Now, spill."

"My pleasure," Ace said. She planted hands on hips. "It's about gold."

"Gold?" all five said together.

Ace grinned. "With a little coaching from Quack, you five could take a comedy act to vaudeville. You'd have them rolling in the aisles. You'd make a mint."

"C'mon, Ace. Spill. Wot's the story about gold?" Gooper said.

"All right, all right. There's a cache of gold ingots on the far side of Sius. Ottoman piracy, I have no doubt. A kind of retirement bonus for somebody like Ernst Heber, perhaps. Somehow, Marilyn Murchison found out about it. She's trying to dig it out and take it. Speaking of piracy, she is up against quite a dastardly pirate in Bengt Braun. Between them, they've got gold fever, and bad."

Sam said, "Bengt Braun was on the *Sea Leopard*?"

"Yes, but I'm afraid that he and his getaway ship have both disappeared. I don't know what he's up to, but whatever it is, it won't be good."

The lanky Tombstone emitted a long whistle of appreciation. "So we gotta git to the far side of the island, pronto!"

"Yeah … pronto …," faintly echoed Bert. He cast his eyes toward the restless volcano and the furlong of water between where he stood and the main island.

Quack also shot a nervous glance at the water. "Uh, I didn't bring my swimming trunks."

"Oh? This could get embarrassing. I'll just wait for you, yonder, shall I?" Ace said in droll tones. Stifling laughter, Ace shallow-dived into the sea like a porpoise and cavorted back to the main island.

Chapter 19

By the time her associates made it to Sius proper, Ace wore her flight suit, dry and comfortable. The coverall sported neat patches at torso and leg. She sat on a blob of congealed lava and watched them splash out of the Mediterranean, stripped down to their skivvies. Their gear was piled in a rubber raft that they towed behind them.

Sheepishly, they dressed. Quack said, "Sam thought of the inflatable raft, back in New York. We'd be sunk without him, just about literally."

"Good work, Sam," Ace said. Sam colored even darker than his usual umber skin tones.

They wedged the raft between a convenient pair of boulders and set off. As they trekked, the associates were amazed to see impala, dik-diks, gazelle, and giraffes. Uncharacteristically, Ace flagged, bringing up the rear. She soldiered on, head down.

"Are there lions?" Sam wondered, round-eyed.

"That would be a 'yes,'" Ace answered darkly. Her hand strayed to touch her ribcage.

"H-how many rifles do we have?" Sam wondered, eyes growing even rounder.

Tombstone volunteered, "Ah brought one."

Gooper said, "An' me. But it's small caliber. It ain't goin' ter stop a *Panthera leo*!"

Ace reassured Gooper and Sam, "In a group, we

should be safe from lions."

Quack said, "This is a switch. Usually, Bert's the predator."

"Careful, you hack. I'm armed." Bert patted a holster at his hip.

Ace said, "It's at least ten miles to the eastern point, as the crow flies, fifteen for us on foot. We won't make it all the way today."

Sam had his brown eye on Ace. He dropped back to march side by side with her. He said softly, "Lady Ace. Usually, I am the slowest in the group. Are you hurt badly?"

"I'm battered, Sam, but I'll live. Thanks for being concerned."

As twilight fell, they stopped in a clearing and made camp. A group of small, curious monkeys gathered around the party as they pitched tents and started a campfire. Gooper warned them not to leave anything small lying around and to especially watch the food items. The monkeys were mottled in shades of brown and tan and had lively eyes framed in light tufts of fur almost like an owl.

Gooper lured one closer with a dried banana slice. The monkey came, and he saw the primate up close. His eyes widened, and he began waving and pointing. His thick accent grew thicker. "Oy! Discovery, says I! It's like *Trachypithecus obscurus*, o' th' Malay peninsula, otherwise known as a dusky leaf monkey, but th' frill 'round th' eyes is diff'rent, an' it's bigger! Hoo! Can't b'lieve it! It's a new species, I'm tellin' yeh! It's not from Africa. I think it's native to Sius!"

Tombstone said dourly, "It's jest a monkey, no matter how many extra Latin names you give it."

But Gooper was so giddy with joy Tombstone could make no dent in his mood.

Ace rested on a lump of lava, grateful to be still. But her calm interlude lasted only a minute. "Ow!" she exclaimed. She leapt up and hopped around on one foot, clawing at her trouser leg.

"Ace? What is it?" Quack said.

Ace pinched an ant off the skin of her lower leg then shook the squashed remains at Quack. Her face twisted in anguish, and her voice cracked. "A siafu ant! Augh!"

All the associates stared at her. This outburst would be perfectly normal for almost anybody, but not Ace.

Sam said, "Are you all right, Lady Ace?"

Ace flicked the dead ant away and closed her eyes. "Breathe, Ace, breathe."

Gooper blew through his bushy mustache. "A siafu ant? One o' them African carnivorous ants? Blimey."

Ace opened her eyes, vastly calmer. "The very same, Gooper. I can't stand them."

"Aye, m'lady."

Ace shuddered. "I don't think I'll be able to sleep tonight."

Bert said, "Carnivorous ants?"

Quack said, "They feed on animals?"

Gooper nodded vigorously. "Animals an' people. There must be a nest nearby."

Quack said, "I don't think I can sleep now, either."

Gooper held up his beefy hands, palms out. "Now, 'old on. There's a remedy."

Ace ceased rubbing her bitten leg and squinted suspiciously at Gooper. "Remedy?"

Gooper said, "Yeh, absolutely. Birds eat these ants,

roight? So ants fear birds. Ants, they can't see sharp, but they can smell. Wot we do is sprinkle some guano aroun' the camp. The ants won't come near."

Ace said, in tones full of wonder, "Gooper, you're a genius."

Tombstone muttered, "Fer the record, he is *not*."

Bert shifted his weight from one foot to the other. "Guano … as in bird poo?"

Tombstone said loudly, "Lemme jes' say I am *not* volunteerin' fer whatever this ginger blowhard is about to propose."

Gooper stuck his tongue out at Tombstone. "Fine, mister beanpole. You cook while we go get some guano. I noticed some rocks by the shore where birds nest. It's a two-minute walk."

Bert said, "But. No. Bird poo?"

Gooper blew air through his mustache at Bert. "Yew c'n wash up. Lots o' water here. A whole sea full o' water."

Ace smiled, her teeth brilliant in the twilight. "I feel like a weight has been lifted from my … my *life*!"

Bert opened his mouth then closed it when Ace smiled. He sighed. "All right. Poo it is. Let's go."

Half the party trudged off to scrape guano from the rocks. They transported the dry but fragrant material to the camp in cupped hands. Careful to leave no gaps, they sprinkled it around the camp perimeter then washed up. No further word of complaint spilled from their lips, not even Bert's.

At supper, Gooper offered tidbits of food to the friendly dusky leaf monkeys. One jumped on his shoulder. Gooper cooed, "Aww! 'E likes me!"

This cozy arrangement worked out well, until

Gooper ran out of the dried banana chips he was offering. The monkey on Gooper's shoulder rode quietly for a while. When no more food was offered, it grew more agitated.

Then the monkey emitted a loud growl. An unearthly, chilling, haunting growl that instantly brought a cold sweat and raised the hackles. A growl that all there had heard before, twinging along their spines when Marilyn Murchison had been kidnapped amid a volley of smoke bombs. A growl heard moments before the associates were gassed at Marilyn Murchison's house. A growl that Ace had heard when the mercenary Stennis was stabbed and tossed overboard.

CHAPTER 20

All of them paled in shock then slumped in dumb-founded surprise.

Finally, Bert broke the silence. "So. One of these monkeys was in New York."

"Wif the gang wot kidnapped Marilyn Murchison," Gooper added.

"The personal pet of Bengt Braun himself, I have little doubt," Ace said. "I guess Braun stood on the sidewalk with a big umbrella, with his monkey hidden beneath."

Tombstone stroked his stubble. "Wull, tie me to a post an' brand my hiney! It was one o' these li'l guys? They shore got a big sound fer such an itty-bitty body."

Gooper shooed the monkey away.

Thankfully, it did not growl again.

Dawn came, sullen and noisy. Eastern rays from the rising sun sidelit a billowy plume of ash that gushed upward from Mt. Sisuvius. Fine ash sifted down over the island, including the Carroway party as they marched eastward. The rumblings and shakings of the mountain grew more and more frequent.

They drew near the site of the tunnel and the *Sea Leopard*. As they wound over the last ridge, an additional staccato sound rose over the increasingly urgent rumbles of the volcano.

"Gunfire," Tombstone said worriedly.

They accelerated as much as they could in the rugged terrain. Huffing with exertion, they crested the last large spur of lava. From this high vantage, they could see a ship nosing toward the docked *Sea Leopard*. The newcomer was larger, darker, and less rusty. Lettering across the bow read "*Cuttlefish*." Muzzle flashes blinked from spots on its deck. The crew of the *Sea Leopard* defended their ship, armed with pistols. But the *Cuttlefish* steadily closed the distance, contemptuous of the meager resistance.

"Cor!" Gooper marveled.

"Anybody have clever ideas, or should we just charge in?" Ace's forehead wrinkled in perplexity.

"Charging in sounds perfect to me! Let's repel some pirates!" Quack said.

"I hope I remember how this works." Sam eyed the gun in his hand as if it were an unsolved cryptogram.

Bert said, "Point and squeeze, Sam. You'll be fine."

Tombstone's keen eyes raked the landscape. "Make fer the *Sea Leopard*. I think there's a path to it where you're not in sight from that there *Cuttlefish*."

"All right. I'll try to find Miss Murchison. Charge!" Ace launched herself downslope.

"Keep your heads down, sahibs."

The five associates followed, angling toward the *Sea Leopard* as the *Cuttlefish* drew closer and closer.

The pirates spotted the newcomers as they darted between trees and boulders. A few shots fired from the *Cuttlefish* pinged against basalt boulders next to the Carroway party.

The distance between the ships narrowed as the associates pounded up the gangplank of the *Sea Leopard*. Bert shouted, "Don't shoot! We're the good guys!"

Captain Landstrad, Harpstone, Lucky, and Turnbull gaped as the five weaved their way on deck and crouched behind cover. "Who're you lot?" demanded Landstrad.

"The wild west cavalry, come in the nick o' time!" Gooper crowed.

Landstrad squinted at them all then bawled, "Permission to come aboard! Now, save me ship!"

Quack said, "That's the idea!"

Bert said, "Ready? Let's give 'em a volley!"

They all popped up from behind their various shelters and fired enthusiastic but wild bullets at the looming *Cuttlefish*'s deck. Pirate heads ducked. Tombstone plugged a couple of shots through the wheelhouse window.

Quack rose from behind a rusted capstan to squeeze off a round or two, but as an incoming bullet clanged off metal, he gave a choked cry. Spinning back to the deck, he leaned against the capstan and clapped a hand to his upper arm.

Bert yowled, "Quack!" He leapt sideways and tucked into a diving roll across the deck. Bullets whizzed by him, but none connected, and he rolled into Quack's shelter.

Quack glanced at his arm. Blood dripped between his clenched fingers. He forced a grin at Bert. "Hey, Bert. No worry. Just a graze, I think."

Bert said, "It had better be!" He reached about

halfway to Quack's injured arm then asked, "What do I do?"

"I wish I could think of a joke answer. Just tie a bandana around it, tight."

"Wicked good."

Sam called over, "Is Mr. Quack all right?"

Bert called back, "Yah, just a graze. More's the pity."

Quack rolled his eyes, then grimaced and hissed at Bert, "Ow! Not so tight!"

"Shh. I'm saving your life. Big baby."

"Shyster."

"Charlatan."

Under the barrage of bullets from the *Sea Leopard*, the pirates stayed mostly out of sight behind obstacles on their own deck. The *Cuttlefish* itself, however, loomed ever closer. A pirate appeared for a moment, flinging a tubular object in a high arc toward the *Sea Leopard*.

"Grenade!" Sam bleated.

"Tarnation! It's one o' them gas grenades, Ah bet!"

The grenade fell short and landed in the water between the ships. The spot where the metal tube sank boiled furiously, erupting blueish vapors.

Quack peered over his capstan shelter. "That's a miss. But they'll get our range soon."

Bert said, "And then we'll be breathing poison."

Captain Landstrad sent the men a wild, popeyed stare. "Poison gas, now?"

Gooper brandished his rifle and bellowed, "Let's stop 'em, then! Fire away! Make 'em turn an' run!"

Tombstone grinned. "Lunatic Brit."

The crew of the *Sea Leopard* and the Carroway party

blazed away with their guns, whooping and yelling.

Not a pirate showed themselves on deck, and the *Cuttlefish* drove forward inexorably.

"We're doomed," Sam said. He hunkered down to reload his pistol. His fingers fumbled, and he dropped several cartridges.

"They're in grenade range," Quack said. "Should we run?"

Clearly, retreat was the wisest course.

Not a man among them moved, however. Young Harpstone paled a trifle.

A new sound burst on their ears. A ratta-tat-tat staccato rattled from down by the beach. A new hail of bullets spattered against the *Cuttlefish*'s metal, ricocheting and banging on the plates in sudden cacophony. There was a wailing screech of pain from aboard the pirate vessel.

Landstrad said, "About time those lazy dogs helped. That's Clout's big gun." He rose and took a shot at a pirate. The crew of the *Cuttlefish* could find few hiding places that kept them safe from both beach and *Sea Leopard*.

"Keep them pinned!" encouraged Sam.

"But keep behind cover, too!" Quack advised.

The *Cuttlefish* came about, prow pointing to the beach, more broadside to the *Sea Leopard*. In this way, the thick steel of the hull deflected the machine gun bullets.

Bert squinted around the corner of a deck housing at the deck of the *Cuttlefish*. "Tombstone," he said, between bursts of machine gun fire, "Look, there."

"Whut, pardner?" Tombstone said as he reloaded.

"I see a loose grenade on top of a barrel. Can you

put a hole in it?"

"Hot horny toads, son! Lemme see!" Tombstone laid his rifle over a crate and pointed it where Bert's finger stabbed. A new fusillade of bullets whistled between the ships. Despite the danger, Tombstone's body flowed and relaxed along his long-barreled rifle.

Harpstone finished reloading and saw Tombstone's performance. "What's he—?"

Quack responded to Harpstone, "Tombstone was a sharpshooter in the Great Wa—"

Tombstone's rifle spoke.

Venting bluish vapor and hissing like an angry snake, the target grenade skittered around the *Cuttlefish*'s deck.

"Oh, well done, Tombstone!" Bert said.

On the *Cuttlefish*, the pirates cried, "Masks! Masks!"

All the gunfire ceased. The *Cuttlefish*'s engines clashed and revved. Its progress reversed.

"They're running away!" Bert said.

"We d-did it!" Harpstone said.

"'At's the way to rumble the ruck!" Gooper said.

The invisible beach machine gun kept up for a few more volleys then quieted. The *Cuttlefish* retreated in earnest. Gooper and Tombstone, the ones with rifles, squeezed off a shot or two, but soon a quiet descended on the whole scene.

Sam addressed Captain Landstrad, "Sahib, we are from Carroway and Associates in New York. It is our pleasure to have been able to assist you in thwarting injustice."

"Eh?" grunted Captain Landstrad. "I mean, thank ye! I was getting worried. Their crew is a dozen or more, it looked like."

"I can't believe we drove 'em off!" crowed Harpstone.

"Piracy waren't inna me contract!" Landstrad's craggy face flushed under his sea tan, and his fists balled up.

Gooper was staring at the *Cuttlefish*, now parked in the middle distance. "Tombstone? What're they doing?"

Tombstone stared, too. "I'll be ding-nabbed if I c'n figger. What is that, anyways?" the lanky Texan replied.

Everybody squinted at the odd goings-on as a small crane swung around on the deck and the crew swarmed around the area. The crane pulled up an object shaped like a cigar. It had fins at the back.

"Oh, no," Quack breathed.

"That is a torpedo, is it not, sahib?" glumly asked Sam.

Chapter 21

Captain Landstrad shouted, "Cast off! Cast off! Start the engines!" Lucky and Harpstone leapt ashore to untether the *Sea Leopard* from its rocky berth.

Turnbull lumbered aft to see about waking up the dormant engines, shaking his head. "Nar. The tanks are cold as a corpse. It'll take half an hour to build up steam."

Even as the sailors scurried, the distant crew of the *Cuttlefish* lowered the torpedo into the water. They aimed it carefully. Throwing a puff of frothed water into the air, the torpedo was on its way.

"Abandon ship! Abandon ship!" Landstrad screamed.

Turnbull pelted down the gangplank just in time. A ka-whump throbbed through the air. The *Sea Leopard* rose into the air several feet. When it fell, jets of water fountained skyward in apparent slow motion. Those on the lava spur threw themselves on the ground as seawater rained in torrents from the sky.

Drenched, they picked themselves up and watched in horrified silence as the *Sea Leopard* ponderously wallowed to one side. Inexorably, it sank. It hit bottom while a corner of the deck was still above water, and there it rested.

The dripping men lined up on the lava spur.

After a lengthy silence, Gooper gripped Landstrad on the shoulder, giving him a gentle but irresistible shake. "That's quite the load of old pony, Cap'n. Condolences."

The *Cuttlefish* steamed north and was soon lost to view around the headlands of Sius. After an hour, it had not come back.

Accompanied by the five associates, the benumbed crew of the *Sea Leopard* staggered off the lava spur. They joined a watchful Clout by her camouflaged beach machine-gun emplacement. She raked her eyes over the five strangers and spat off to one side. Ace, a hatless, frazzled Marilyn Murchison, and an energized bald Garbruck arrived at the same moment.

Ace scanned the incoming men. "None of you are injured?"

Captain Landstrad passed a weary hand over his eyes then jabbed a thumb at Quack. "Jeest that blond lad."

Quack raised his chin nobly. "A mere scratch. Hello, Miss Murchison."

"Oh my!" the actress cried. She flew to Quack and slipped a hand to his shoulder. She stared at the red-soaked bandana as Quack's lips lifted in a smile.

"You know," said Bert stiffly, "He's really quite brave. For an actor."

Quack lifted an eyebrow at Bert. Bert smirked back.

Murchison glanced at Bert. "Oh, so are you. So are *all* of you. I never meant for any of this to happen."

With eyes shining, Harpstone blurted, "Hey! That

Mutt Maloney guy went down with the ship! He's dead!"

Everyone glanced at Harpstone, but no one dredged up sufficient sympathy to compose an elegy for the drowned assassin.

Ace said, "Clout. Garbruck. These are my five associates. We're here to help." The golden flyer squared off, facing the actress. She raised an eyebrow and planted fists on hips. "I think your crew deserves some straight answers now."

Marilyn winced. Her eyes glanced to Quack's bloodstain then dropped. "It's all gone wrong. I'm so sorry." She turned her gaze to Captain Landstrad, a smile lighting up her face. "But even now, it may come out all right. The tunnel is almost clear."

"How," Captain Landstrad wanted to know, "does that help? Me ship just sunk!" His shaking finger stabbed out to sea. "We're trapped on a volcano!" His finger stabbed inland. "And pirates want to kill us!" He drew his finger across his throat.

"It was a secret I thought I would never tell, but I have to spill it now. Here goes." Marilyn took a deep breath then released it in a gush of words. "There are crates of gold stored in there. The Ottomans hid it during the Great War. Not many people knew about it. Until today, only Bengt Braun and I knew. Anyway, if we can get it out, we'll all be rich." Marilyn glanced at Ace, who gave a single nod and a crinkle at the corners of her eyes.

"Oh," Captain Landstrad said faintly. "By gum, that *does* help."

The actress lifted her chin. "We've got to clear those last few boulders! Then we can work on our other problems."

"It's not *that* far to Greece or Italy. Maybe we could build a raft," mused Bert.

Old Lucky wheezed, "Nar. There's a lifeboat left. On the *Sea Leopard*, I mean. Should be seaworthy. Got to cut it free. Got to bail it out."

Mt. Sisuvius rumbled. Everyone felt the vibration thrumming through their feet.

"Um. We should hurry," Garbruck said sourly.

"Right." Marilyn Murchison laid hands on her hairline in agitation. "Garbruck, please get back to the bulldozer. Half of you help Garbruck with dragging rocks out. The other half, get the lifeboat."

Bert and Quack hovered near the actress. With Ace, Garbruck, Lucky, and Captain Landstrad, they went to inspect the progress inside the tunnel. Ace's eyes strayed upward. "That roof can't possibly be stable. Bracing it with timbers would be wise, but I don't suppose there's time."

"We haven't used any dynamite," Marilyn Murchison said. "The bulldozer seemed a lot safer, even if it's slower. But, see? See the darkness through those little spaces? That's the other side! We're almost through. A few more boulders out should make it so there's an opening."

The mercenary, Garbruck, hopped in the bulldozer's driver's seat and pointed. "See them chains? Wrap 'em around the next boulder." He squinted at Quack and Bert. The pair found the proposal a lot less interesting than cozying up to Marilyn Murchison, but they obeyed. Ace pitched in, too. The tunnel soon filled with smoke, dust, and noise as the bulldozer struggled to budge the massive boulders.

Young Harpstone and thick Turnbull, along with Gooper, Sam, and Tombstone, headed for the forlorn wreck of the *Sea Leopard*. Clout stayed with her entrenched machine gun. The lifeboat was easily seen, tied to the *Sea Leopard*, canted over at wave level, and half full of Mediterranean brine. The five men swam and climbed and cursed and grunted. But by degrees, they managed to free the boat. They dragged it up the beach. Weary and wet, they hiked back toward the tunnel.

The bulldozer crawled out of the tunnel. With its front blade, it rolled a boulder out to add it to the impressive pile of excavated rocks that had grown around the tunnel entrance. The dusty diggers paused work to hear the good news about the lifeboat. They reported in turn, "An hour, maybe less, and we'll be able to walk right in."

"Ace!" came a call from the lava spur nearby.

The mysterious voice added, "Don't shoot!" when an array of revolvers was pointed in his direction. It was Yanni. The young Greek was perspiring and breathing hard.

Ace climbed a few steps upslope to meet the young man. "What's the matter, Yanni?"

Yanni spread his hands in supplication. "Ace! My family! They are trying to leave, but a big, black ship came and anchored, blocking their way. The men on board have guns. My parents are afraid to leave, and yet the volcano swells each hour. It will burst very soon! Ace, can you help?"

"I thought ye said this island was deserted?" Captain Landstrad griped to Marilyn Murchison.

Marilyn Murchison stood hypnotized by Yanni's

curly hair, regular features, and sweat-soaked shirt that clung to the sculpted muscles of his chest. She said to the captain without taking her wide eyes from Yanni, "I said that, yes. I guess I was wrong. But so far, the natives seem *quite* friendly."

Yanni glanced at Marilyn for a moment and smiled, despite his distress.

Marilyn tucked a lock of blonde hair behind her ear and smiled back. "Hello … Yanni."

Ace regarded Yanni worriedly then glanced back at the excavation operation. She had not answered Yanni's plea for help.

Sam twirled the end of his mustache. "Lady Ace, we are many now. We can defend this place."

Ace rested her eyes on Sam for a moment. She nodded in the affirmative and turned to Yanni. "All right. I'll see what I can do."

Ace swiveled back to her associates. "Don't go picking fights. If the *Cuttlefish* has anchored, Braun and his party may be coming overland. Best outcome for everybody is if you are gone when he gets here."

Ace sprinted off into the rough terrain. Yanni followed, but only after one lingering, backward glance at Marilyn Murchison.

CHAPTER 22

"Everybody knows Ace, I guess," a bemused Bert remarked.

"Oh, wasn't he something?" breathed Marilyn Murchison. She tore her eyes from the forest and inserted her hands into the elbows of Quack and Bert, who flanked her. "Not that you gentlemen aren't something, too, of course!"

"I'm glad I'm somebody," Quack said with a sigh.

Sam cleared his throat, his hands clasped behind his back. "Might I inquire what the plan is? Are we going to go now? Or stay?"

"Go?" inquired Marilyn Murchison, both eyebrows raising.

"Go?" said Garbruck incredulously.

"There's buried treasure here!" Captain Landstrad cried. "Back to work!" There was a veritable stampede back to the tunnel.

When the commotion faded, Bert, Quack, Gooper, Tombstone, and Sam were left looking at each other owlishly.

Marilyn Murchison gripped Bert's and Quack's elbows and stared in the direction Yanni had gone. She murmured, "Do you ever pause and wish to rethink the choices you made in the past?"

Tombstone answered in a soothing drawl, "Ah think we've just witnessed why you keep your trap shut, iffen you know 'bout hidden treasure. Them varmints in there got gold fever, an' they got it bad! We ain't gonna blame you much fer keepin' quiet 'bout it."

"Yeah!" Bert said.

"For sure!" Quack added.

Sam fingered the curled ends of his mustache. "Miss Murchison, may I ask how you knew of the gold, and how you are connected with Bengt Braun?"

Bert raised a finger in the air. "Before you answer, Miss Murchison, as a lawyer, I have to point out that it is not a crime to be the daughter of a deceased Ottoman minister of the interior. It may be a public relations mistake to write that on your resumé, but it does not reflect upon your inner character."

The actress gasped. "You already knew? Oh my!"

"Tricky shyster!" Quack accused. He assured the blonde, "We only guessed. We *did* investigate, of course. We do run a detective agency."

"Well, it's true. I found out about this island when I went through some of my father's old papers. I knew about Bengt Braun. He is a steamer captain now, but during the war, he was an Ottoman navy captain. Not warships. Other ships. I thought I could trust him." Murchison sighed and shook her head ruefully.

"There, there," Quack soothed.

"It's all right," Bert cooed.

"Yew two're makin' me nauseous," Gooper grumbled.

"Anyway, I hired him to take me here. We blasted the gates open, and he saw what was inside: many wooden crates full of gold ingots. He wanted more pay, at first. Then he wanted a quarter share of the gold. Then he demanded a half share. I realized then

121

he would take the whole lot if he could. The way he talked and acted, well, I began to fear for my own safety! I'm no Ace Carroway, to win a fight with such a big, strong man. I was in a tight spot."

"Wot did yeh do?" Gooper asked.

Marilyn compressed her lips. "I set off the rest of the dynamite in the tunnel. The tunnel collapsed."

"Braun must've been madder'n a mama bear two cubs short!" Tombstone mused.

The actress grimaced. "I played innocent. I didn't say a word. Perhaps he thought I was not capable of doing it. Perhaps I really am a good actress. Anyway, he did not suspect me. When he finished shouting and stomping, he took me back to New York."

"To gear up for a second crack at it, huh?" Quack guessed.

Marilyn sighed. "Yes. But then I got too clever for my own good. One night, I dressed in black and broke into his house. I deposited one of my paintings, and I stole one of his smoking pipes."

"Oh! Well, that's a surprise!" Quack said. "Your painting really wasn't stolen from your house, at all?"

"No. I stole my own painting, I guess you'd say. After the police finished with me, I came to see you at Carroway and Associates. I was hoping you would find the painting and send Captain Braun to jail. What I managed to do, instead, was tip him off that I was working against him."

"Well, at least you met us!" Bert said, patting her hand and smiling.

"Yes! That's a bright spot!" The actress's smile dazzled.

Tombstone let out a long whistle. "I'll be hornswoggled. It took a lot o' nerve, reverse-stealin' a painting."

Marilyn Murchison had the grace to blush.

Sam said, "I think we should leave, right now. I think we should forget the gold and leave before we are covered in lava or shot."

"Wot's this 'ere surge o' caution in yew, Sam? Where's yer sense o' adventure?" Gooper scoffed. "Come on, you lot! Let's get ter clearin' out stone."

The estimate of an hour was optimistic. Three hours later, the bulldozer dragged the last large boulder out of the way. The men shifted rubble to clear a person-sized opening. There was a cheer, "We're through!"

In their single-mindedness, they ignored the ever-more frequent tremors of the volcano and palpable sense of mounting tension as explosive forces grew and grew underground.

Sam heard a faint pop sound from outside the cave. "What was that? It sounded like a shot!"

Garbruck cackled madly. "A shot, eh? Well, if they're comin', let's give 'em a reception they won't soon forget!" He spun two revolvers in his hands and grinned like a death's head.

The tunnel opening was bright, relatively speaking, though a false twilight had fallen due to the spreading ash cloud overhead. They all minced toward the tunnel exit, scanning for any sign of movement or men from the Braun party. They reached the opening.

Familiar trees and landscape stretched out before them, befogged by a drizzle of falling volcanic ash.

"Bah," Garbruck said. He sent a disgusted sneer to Sam.

"I don't see nothin'!" Harpstone loudly reported.

As if in answer, the air filled with an unearthly growl. A haunting sound that set one's teeth on edge and filled the soul with fearful despair.

"The growling death!" Sam cried.

A volley of silver-gray canisters dropped from above the cave entrance. They hit the rocky ground and hissed like enraged snakes. Plumes of vapor spurted.

"Gas!" yelped Harpstone. He flapped his hands at the fog then toppled. Sam wobbled a few steps down the tunnel then collapsed. One by one, the rest dropped to the gravelly floor. Gooper ran deeper into the tunnel and almost reached the newly made opening, but his shoulders jammed between wall and boulder on the first try, and he didn't get a second attempt. His eyes fluttered shut, and he collapsed on the rubble pile.

CHAPTER 23

Ace and Yanni ran steadily, weaving and dodging over the rough terrain. Ace's cracked rib translated each footfall into a stab of pain. A very long two miles later, Yanni led Ace to a sheltered inlet on the north shore. A patched-up metal boat floated there. A relic of the Great War, it was once a small, motorized utility boat. Lashed together in a small bundle, the household goods of the family lay in the bottom of the boat. A makeshift mast jutted near the bow. Behind a knob of basalt, Steffi and Giocco peeked out at the dark shadow of the *Cuttlefish* that lay a half mile out to sea.

The panting pair chuffed to a halt.

"Ace! Dear, dear Ace!" Steffi threw her arms around the sweaty pilot and squeezed. Ace winced but hugged back anyway, then repeated the process with Giocco.

"We do not know if it is safe! The men had guns. Most of them came ashore," Giocco explained.

"They came ashore, eh? That's bad news for those I left at the tunnel but good news for us. They probably left only a few crewmen on board."

"What are we to do, Ace? Can you help us?" Yanni asked gently.

Ace shook sweat from her eyes and squinted toward the distant ship.

A memory stirred. "See? She strikes!" Siyanda stabbed a pointing finger across the savanna. White teeth gleamed in his

125

dark face, and an eager light was in his eye. Cecilia followed the sight line to watch the unfolding drama. The startled springbok herd flowed in full flight, and the cheetah pursued, kicking up dust clouds with each step. It closed upon the rearmost of the antelope.

Worry stole over Cecilia's face, but she and her tutor were much too far away to affect the outcome. The life and death contest played out. The cheetah leapt upon her target springbok. But the long-legged antelope leaped sideways, and the raking claws scored only tufts of fur. The cheetah landed poorly, raising a new cloud of dust as it slid and rolled. As the dust cleared, it sat tall, licking a paw as if nothing had happened.

"The antelope got away!" Cecilia reported.

"Yes, child. This time."

"Will the cheetah be faster next time?" Cecilia asked, nose wrinkling. This did not seem likely to the six-year-old.

"It depends. But, usually, yes."

"Why? Will the cheetah exercise like me?"

"No, child! But she will get hungry, which you seldom feel in your belly. When you are hungry, you find a way. When what you want becomes what you must have, that is when you find out what you can truly accomplish."

Ace focused on the earnest young man next to her. "Yanni, it will be a pleasure. It's a quarter-hour swim out then a few minutes to secure the ship. I'll wave at you when it's safe to come. When I wave, come quickly. The volcano may erupt any minute."

Ace stripped down to the swimsuit Steffi had given her. She wrapped her flight suit around her boots and tossed the bundle into the Bennetto family's ark.

She dived into the sea.

"What are you going to do?" Steffi asked, but it was too late to get an answer. Ace swam freestyle for a while, then porpoised and disappeared from sight altogether.

Yanni watched her go, his sweating face yearning.

His father laid a hand on Yanni's shoulder. "My son. To hold a star in your hand is more desirable than gold. But stars, they are untouchable."

Grutch slumped inside the wheelhouse of the *Cuttlefish* and stared over at the volcano dozily. The volcano didn't scare him, not from this distance. He preferred to be left behind than to go ashore, anyway.

There was a sudden knock at the door. It startled him. He peered out the door's window. Nothing. Only the dark night. "Norbert? Stop playin' around and get back to sleep! I'm not taking two watches in a row to cover for a lazy sea dog like you."

But there was silence. Norbert was nowhere to be seen. "Bah. Seagull, maybe?" Grutch opened the door and stepped out.

Instantly, a vice gripped his throat and slammed his head back into the bulkhead. His hands flailed, and his eyes focused on a dark, scarred face that studied him intently. The golden eyes bored holes into his soul.

The vision blurred out as Grutch lost consciousness, oxygen flow to his brain choked off by fingers more like metal than flesh.

Yanni cried, "Look!"

Out on the *Cuttlefish*, Ace had turned the electric signal light on herself. Thus spotlighted, she waved to the shore.

"There is a sight to behold," Giocco said.

"We are saved!" Steffi half-sobbed.

In short order, they launched. Yanni and Giocco each rowed. There was some breeze from the west, and Steffi set the sail to catch it.

As they neared the anchored *Cuttlefish*, its engines belched to life.

Ace appeared at the rail to hail the family as they passed. Steffi threw up Ace's bundle of clothes.

"Bon voyage! Kaló taksídi!" called Ace.

"Efxaristo! Thank you!" the Bennetto family called back.

Ace waved one more time then hurried back to work. She reeled the anchor chain through the chock then raced to the engine room to engage the screws. Finally, she ran to the wheelhouse and set a course.

A throbbing boom emanated from the volcano. Showers of red, glowing cinders began raining down. The Bennetto family rowed harder, heading northeast for Greece.

The *Cuttlefish* steamed southeast, around the curve of the island and into the curtain of falling volcanic ash.

CHAPTER 24

Ace anchored the *Cuttlefish* near the sunken *Sea Leopard* but out of sight around the headland. She wanted to leave it in a safer spot farther from the eruption, but her worry about her five associates and Marilyn Murchison drove her to risk it.

She left Grutch and Norbert in the *Cuttlefish*'s brig. Ace was simultaneously thankful and appalled that the *Cuttlefish* was equipped with its own small jail. Was trafficking humans another of Captain Braun's sins?

Ace swam to shore. Wearily, she shambled out of the water. The relentless physical activity and injuries took their toll, even on Ace's elite constitution. She unrolled her battered flight suit and stepped into it and her boots. Over the lava spur she hiked, each step heavy in the acidic air. As her lungs burned and labored, Ace wondered if the volcano's outgassings were poisonous.

Mt. Sisuvius boomed again, much louder. A great cloud of cinders and lava bombs hurtled from its crater. A large bomb crashed not far from Ace, splashing blobs of lava and obliterating several trees. A glowing mass of liquid rock arced toward her. She threw herself to the ground in the nick of time. The lava bomb wiped out grasses and bushes next to Ace, starting fires. The lava's radiant heat baked her on one side, and thorns raked into her flesh on the other.

Despite the heat, she shivered. She picked herself

off the ground with an agonized groan. Something had peppered smoking holes in Ace's flight suit, but she wasn't on fire. As she limped away from the fire, she plucked out the largest of the thorns embedded in her skin.

Each thorn pinched between forefinger and thumb reminded Ace of siafu ants, hard and sharp and impervious to logic. Her weary footfalls echoed those of her hopeless childhood odyssey.

Ace halted, thrills of dread chasing up and down her spine. A silent river of dark red glistened across her path. The fluid ignored gravity and flowed over obstacles. In the dim light, it was difficult to perceive the reality, but Ace knew in the marrow of her bones exactly what it was. Millions of siafu ants marched in a ravenous column. Her childhood nightmare re-formed before her waking eyes.

She glanced longingly back at the bright stripe of placid Mediterranean visible beyond the edge of the ash cloud. The blue ribbon shone with the promise of comfort and safety, free of volcanoes. Free of lava bombs that hurtled from the sky. No pirates. No impossible obligations. No nightmares.

Ace snapped out of the daydream with a bark of laughter. The long scars across her face pulled until she relaxed to a serene expression. "Miss Carroway, that is not the way of the snow leopard. Nor the cheetah. Nor the lesson I learned from the siafu ants when I was, what, nine? I am grown up now."

Mirthlessly, she grinned. "Also, look down, you ninny. You have boots on."

She revolved away from the light, golden eyes spearing toward the primal storm.

She gathered herself like a sprinter. She sprang away, crunching over the insect swarm toward her associates and Marilyn Murchison.

The volcano's constant rumblings killed any need for stealth. Its rim glowed with crawling streams of lava that added fresh crimson to the mountain of blood. A low roaring from unseen gas vents added to the ominous mood. The west wind blew the ash and cinders to fall on the eastern slopes where the tunnel entrance was located. The thick plumes of steam and ash belching from Mt. Sisuvius blotted out the sunny Mediterranean late afternoon sky. Gloom dominated. Most of the scant illumination came from the flickering red glow of the volcano itself.

Ace worriedly approached the tunnel entrance from upslope. The possibilities of what she would find there frightened her. Had the pirates ambushed the Murchison party? She crouched behind a boulder and spied over the top.

She gasped aloud. The jumble of animal cages left by the tunnel entrance had been sorted. People were crammed inside three of the largest. The outlines of hulking Gooper and skeletal Tombstone stood out the clearest. She counted, squinting. All five associates, Miss Murchison, and all four *Sea Leopard* crew members were there. Ace exhaled in relief. Clout and Garbruck, the mercenaries, were in a separate cage.

A thick man in a naval coat stood wide-legged, smoking a pipe and gloating at Marilyn Murchison. His back was to Ace, but even without the monkey on his shoulder, it was obviously Bengt Braun. Ten scruffy, well-armed men gathered around in a loose semicircle. From the belts of each, gas masks dangled.

Ace could barely hear their voices over the volcanic roar.

"Lucky minx. You're a cat with nine lives," the pirate accused smugly, hands on hips as he gloated.

"To think I trusted you!" Murchison said miserably.

"Bah. You hired detectives and put 'em on my trail. You deserve your cage. Where's that Ace woman? She's the only one missing."

"Ace?" gasped Marilyn. "Well, I don't know! But you'd better hope she doesn't catch you!"

Braun cawed. "Oh, haw, haw! Just look around, you dumb wench! Who's in charge now? Me, that's who. Now, shut up. I'm done with you."

Bengt Braun swaggered over to the cage holding Clout and Garbruck. He grunted. "You two are mercs?"

"We're not with them anymore," Clout said.

"We're for hire, plain and simple," Garbruck said.

"Eh? Bloody turncoats!" spat Captain Landstrad from two cages over.

"When we're paid, we're loyal as anything. It's just lookin' like the actress is gonna default on her bill." Clout spat to one side. "I bet you can beat the dame's price by taking a pocketknife and shaving a few flakes off of one of them gold bars in there."

There was an immediate, electric reaction from the semicircle of gun-toting hirelings. "Gold? What? What'd she say? Gold bars?" They stirred with sudden aggression, swiveling to face the captain and his monkey.

Bengt Braun bared his teeth, glaring from man to man. "Gold? Gold, you wanna know? Well, the answer's yes! And if you want your cut, you'd better listen to me and do what I say double quick. You!" Braun stabbed a finger at a man with a rifle. "Watch these cages, and shoot whoever gives you any sass."

Braun wheeled back to Clout and Garbruck's cage. "You two, welcome to the crew. I've got my eye on you. We keep your guns, but if you keep your noses clean, I'll see you get your fair wages." He slid back a pair of bolts, and the mercenaries crawled from the animal cage.

The caged prisoners muttered, but all the guns in evidence persuaded them to keep their rebellion at a simmer.

Braun shot blistering stares at his crew, one by one. "Listen, you lot. The gold comes in crates, and I want the crates out whole. The hole's not big enough for that yet, so get in there and start chipping! Move it! I'll whip anybody that shirks. Lazy cutthroats!"

Mt. Sisuvius boomed and kicked mightily. The ground beneath their feet heaved. All the pirates stumbled, and a few hit the dirt. Rocks fell from the tunnel roof, their crashes reverberating in the tunnel. Braun's monkey screeched and scampered away into the woods.

After the echoes of falling rock faded, Braun waved his pistol in the air and thundered, "Get in there, you bad excuses! You want to be rich as a baron? Go dig."

Nine men, plus Garbruck and Clout, scurried off into the tunnel. Braun swaggered in the rear like a bull among sheep.

The instant Braun was out of sight, Ace moved. Braun had left but a single guard.

Cinders pelted the area, thudding around like hot, rocky rain. Many parts of the forest were smoking ominously, with open flames blazing here and there.

Ace moved into a position behind the nervous guard. Casting around, she laid hands on a hefty hunk of loose lava. "This doesn't seem very sporting," Ace murmured, hefting the rock in her hand.

Ace waited for the right moment then lobbed the rock. It arced with mathematical precision through the air. With a hollow thunk, it connected with the guard's skull. He dropped like a mood on Monday.

Ace sprinted forward but paused to check on the guard's condition. Ace concluded that no further abuse was necessary. The fellow would be out for a while.

She scuttled forward toward the cages, where grins of welcome were lighting up.

She was just about there when her eye caught movement in the tunnel. Ace swerved and slid behind a cage. Ace whispered, "Gooper, you make a better door than a window—for which I am eternally grateful."

"Ace! I am jubilant ter see yew!" Gooper rumbled. He continued to speak, narrating under his breath. "It's Clout comin' out. She's saunterin' all full o' swagger.

"Now she's pickin' up speed, maybe goin' ter stop at the guard. Oh, no, she kept goin'. She's runnin', plain an' simple. Runnin' ter the beach. Oh, wait, somebody else is coming out of the—"

A gunshot popped.

Bengt Braun's irate voice screamed, "There! That'll serve you, wench! Tryin' to steal my gold? Argh!"

The caged people quivered and gasped. Marilyn Murchison cried softly, "Oh no! Oh, please, no!"

Harpstone gulped. "Shot 'er in the back!"

Braun's footsteps crunched toward the fallen guard. "Huh? What's the matter with you? Get up!" There was a soft thump of boot striking flesh and a pitter-patter up a tree that overhung the cages. Braun muttered, "He's knocked out? What is this?"

Braun stomped toward the cages with great agitation, his enraged face purple and monstrous. "You people did that, somehow, didn't you? Or was it the volcano? Either way, I can't watch you all, so I'm puttin' you out of your misery." He cocked his rifle. Aiming from the hip, he pointed the muzzle at the first person in the cage, from left to right. That first person was Marilyn Murchison.

It happened too fast. Ace could not react in time.

Braun's finger tightened on the trigger.

The ground shifted in a paroxysm of active geology. Braun's feet were shifted to the left. The shot rang, followed by the zing of a ricochet and the rattle of the metal of the cage.

"Oh!" Marilyn breathed, realizing that she had by a hairsbreadth escaped a bullet meant for her. But Braun recovered his balance and aimed again. From her point of view, the long barrel of the rifle foreshortened to a gray-rimmed black dot.

Ace fell out of the sky. When his attention had been on the unconscious guard, she had whisked up the overhanging tree. Boots first, she landed on Braun.

The impact sent him sprawling backward with a squawk. Ace hit the ground rolling, then found her feet and launched herself at Braun.

The pirate captain staggered upright. "You! Ace Carroway!" Bending, he grabbed the barrel of his rifle from the dirt and swung the stock at Ace's face.

Ace ducked under the swing and stiff-armed Braun in the stomach. He flew backward, his rifle spinning away, airborne.

"Yes. You found me. Why aren't you happy?" Ace wondered sardonically. She stalked toward the gasping pirate as he struggled to his feet, a hand clapped to her own ribcage.

"Get him, Ace!" Quack cheered from the cage.

Braun snarled and threw a right hook toward Ace's jaw.

Ace caught his fist in her palm and used his own momentum to spin him. A boot in his midback sent him sailing several yards. His midair squeal abruptly stopped as he landed on his face on the rocky ground. He lay motionless.

Ace raced to the cages and unbolted them.

"Rescued! Amazing!" Harpstone half-sobbed.

But before the cages were empty, the whole world split apart. The very earth itself jerked to one side, and everyone sprawled to the ground, even Ace. Trees splintered and fell. The sky lit up in an explosion of crimson.

The roaring of the volcano so assaulted their ears that no one could hear anyone else. They staggered and reeled to their feet.

Ace stood, too. With her arm, she pointed urgently toward the beach. She picked up Braun's discarded rifle and kept a watch on the tunnel entrance, which was full of airborne dust. The tunnel dust started to glow orange-red, flickering and brightening. The crew and associates all stumbled for the beach and the life-boat moored there.

Ace backpedaled, playing rearguard. Braun dragged

himself to his knees and glared. A dizzied man staggered out of the tunnel, holding his head with both hands. Braun dragged himself erect, stabbed a finger at the dizzied man, and screamed above the din, "Get back in there, coward!" The hapless crewman stumbled on, giving no sign that he had heard. Braun stomped toward him and smashed him into the ground with his pile driver fists.

The tunnel was no longer a dark, gloomy hole. It shone with a bright orange glow, becoming brighter. As Braun stepped toward the tunnel, the source of the glow moved outward. A galloping tongue of molten rock filled the tunnel from floor to ceiling. The bulldozer and some boulders danced at its front edge, tumbling over and over. Then all was engulfed by the hellishly glowing liquid.

Braun screamed in primal terror and flailed in a panic to run away, but the wall of lava poured over him, and he disappeared in a flash of fire.

"Faster!" Ace urged as flaming cinders fell all around them.

Chapter 25

Ace skidded to a stop at the facedown body of Clout. She felt for a pulse. She frowned.

"Ace! Come on!" shouted Quack, his voice a whisper compared to the roar of the volcano.

With the heat of the oncoming wall of lava blistering her back, Ace dug her shoulder under the body then hefted the mercenary to her shoulders in a fireman's carry. Ace roared in agony as her broken rib-ends grated. She strained to move her leaden feet in the heat-shimmery air, all too aware of the onrushing lava and the burning trees that lay between her and the beach.

At first, the lava gained. Its first touch on her heels would mean her death.

She sprinted mightily. The heat receded. The danger lessened with each step. She left the tongue of lava behind. The lava flow fanned out to fill the flat space, and its forward progress slowed.

Ace's associates, the crew of the *Sea Leopard*, and Marilyn crossed the crescent beach and piled into the lifeboat. Ace dumped the limp body of Clout into the boat. Many hands helped her tumble over the gunwales to relative safety. She lay for a moment in the bottom, breathing hard.

"I'm alive!" she crowed.

Quack and Bert were the last in after pushing the lifeboat off the beach. Gooper and Tombstone manned the oars, pulling with gusto.

The lava tongue overran the beach machine gun emplacement. The ammunition exploded like demonic popcorn.

Cinders continued to fall around them, hissing in the water. Several landed among them, bouncing painfully off human bodies to splash and hiss in the water pooled in the bottom of the boat.

As the slow lifeboat passed the wreck of the *Sea Leopard*, the lava river touched the sea. A steam cloud burst forth with an angry teakettle scream.

The noise level gradually tapered off. Among the escaping passengers, there were several burns and countless bruises. People coughed ash out of their lungs. But not a one complained. Not after a glance shoreward, where steam hissed and billowed, lava glowed, and trees ignited in brilliant pillars of flame.

Evening approached. Ace directed the rowers north. Mt. Sisuvius loomed aglow with traceries of lava flows cascading down its sides. It wore a crown of titanic fireworks as the barrage of cinders and bombs continued.

"Cor! Never seen the like," Gooper muttered.

Quack said, "'I am amazed, and know not what to say.'"

Bert winced. "That was Shakespeare, wasn't it?"

Quack said, "Yes, it was. But I think even the bard could find no words adequate for this."

The cove and the wreck of the *Sea Leopard* slipped out of sight, and the *Cuttlefish* hove into view. The falling of cinders abated.

Marilyn Murchison watched the dark ship, her mouth a tight line. "Will they rescue us or shoot us?"

Ace said, "No one is on deck. There are two crew, and they are in the brig. We'll have the ship to ourselves."

An astonished Captain Landstrad said, "Yer a bloody miracle worker, that's what ye are! Ye collared the crew and sailed her over here?"

"That is our Lady Ace!" Sam said, rubbing at a cinder burn on his leg.

"Why'd you bring the body, Ace?" Quack said, reaching down to touch Clout's body. He answered himself, "Oh! She's alive."

He investigated further. "I see. The bullet creased her head. Plenty of blood, but she'll probably recover. Possibly concussed. I suppose she'll wake up pretty woozy. Still, I'd better frisk her for more knives and guns."

"You shoulda left her," young Harpstone said, sullenly.

A thoughtful Marilyn Murchison answered, "No. No, Harpstone. Not that Clout is worth a plugged nickel, but it's better this way, even if it's less convenient." The actress glanced at Ace. "I think I understand Ace Carroway now. She'd have rescued even that rat Bengt Braun, if that had been possible."

Meanwhile, Quack had been searching Clout. He exclaimed, "Whoa!" and held up a metal ingot. The red lights of Mt. Sisuvius reflected from its glossy sides as he turned it this way and that. All eyes riveted to the bar of gold.

"I'm sure you'll find quite a few of those on her person," Ace said drily. "She was very, very heavy to carry."

Chapter 26

Captain Landstrad and his crew took charge of the *Cuttlefish*, and they charted a wide, safe circle around Sius to the western islet. At such a comfortable distance, the deadly volcano became a graceful and beauteous paragon of nature.

The five associates, Ace, and Marilyn Murchison watched the show amidships. They drank coffee from tin cups, and all the injured had fresh bandages.

"Can I go with you, in your airship?" Marilyn asked. There was a subtle yearning in her voice.

"Oh, may she?" Quack jumped in.

"Certainly," Ace said.

"Can we go to Greece? And is that family going to be all right?" Marilyn wondered.

Ace said, "Greece? Yes. The winds are generally blowing that way. It's easiest to go where the wind takes us. And the family? They will be fine. Did I explain about the ventilation shafts?"

"No!"

"Ah. Well, we've been short on time. The Ottomans drilled ventilation shafts down into the gold storage room. Yanni showed them to me on the hillside above his house. They were large enough, barely, for a person to slip through, and so I borrowed a rope and explored. The far wall of the chamber was hot, and I could hear molten rock moving. But I also found the crates of ingots."

Marilyn blinked. "You found the gold? Amazing. And then you just left it there."

Ace shook her head. "No, I took some. With what I gave them, the Bennetto family should be off to a decent new start as they reenter civilization."

The actress gushed, "Ace! My goodness! You amaze me yet again! So selfless, never thinking of yourself, always taking care of others! I'm a better person after getting to know you and your men. I think I will donate to an orphanage or a hospital when I get back to New York!"

Ace smiled lopsidedly. "Who says I didn't think about myself? I kept some, too. I'm thinking of using it to build an airship factory."

"Ah wondered what was in that bundle y'all stowed under th' tarp at th' airship." Tombstone grinned. "Why din't cha tell us?"

"It wasn't relevant." Ace sipped coffee. "We were solving a mystery and trying to keep Marilyn alive."

"Alive! I'll drink to that!" the actress said. They all clinked tin cups.

By the whims of the prevailing west wind, no cinders or lava bombs fell on the canvas-covered airship. Under Ace's direction, the associates attached a large net to the wheeled gondola. Ace fired up a small chemical plant that combined silicol with hot, concentrated caustic soda to fill three gasbags, each held inside the net and arranged in a line like a bloated ellipsis. The triple-bagged affair looked antique but functional, despite Ace's grousing about poor engineering and inefficiency[5].

Soon, the airship became lighter than air, straining at its tether, yearning for the sky. Ace, Marilyn Murchison, and the five associates boarded the gondola. Lazily, they floated up off the ground.

The *Cuttlefish* steamed off. Captain Landstrad tried to puzzle out whether he could claim her as salvage or if he was guilty of piracy in taking her. Legal gray areas aside, however, Ace had given each crew member one of Clout's stolen ingots of gold. And each dreamed of bright futures far from the seaways.

Mt. Sisuvius had quieted. The airship floated northeast toward Greece at the whim of the air currents. A propeller and engine comprised the rear of the gondola, but Ace kept them inert, preferring to sail the airways in silence.

Marilyn Murchison kept her face glued to the forward windows, straining to see glimpses of Grecian shores. Bert and Quack glumly noted her obsessive gazing. Independently, they concluded that their own charms did not compare to those of a wide-eyed, curly-haired young Greek who wanted to see the world.

"Come on, Bert," said Quack. "I brought dice. Let's play some craps or something."

"All right. What's the wager?"

"Wager? Hmm. Oh, I know! Winner gets the next hot canary who comes through the agency doors, with

---

[5] She had designed and built it from car parts and a fisherman's net, so perhaps she spoke with some authority.

no interference by third wheels."

"Ha! You're on."

Gooper stirred. "Wot? Wait! Oi'm in!"

Tombstone said, "An' me!"

Sam's curled mustache rocked back and forth. "Hot canary? I am familiar with the dice game craps, but I do not know why there is such interest in heated birds."

Tombstone said, "Son, sometime I'll jes' have to 'xplain the facts of life to ya. Fer now, though, come on in. Let's see how *hot* you kin make yer dice."

The dice game in the rear of the little gondola grew noisy. Ace lounged at the helm, wearing a dreamy half-smile as the air carried them along.

Marilyn shot Ace a worried glance. She whispered, "What will become of me?"

Ace wrinkled her brow. "I don't follow."

"You know I'm Ernst Heber's daughter. I'm at your mercy. One newspaper exposé and I'd be run out of the country."

"Oh."

"Also, I'm a liar. And stupid. I almost got you and your men killed. I almost got *myself* killed!"

"True. Even after the time bomb exploded, you were feeding me fiction."

"You could tell? I'm not the actress I thought I was."

"Your acting was fine, but your playwright left logic holes in your script."

"What will it be, then?" Marilyn's chin lifted proudly, but also a tremor ran through her. She gazed at Ace with eyes ashimmer.

Ace reached out and squeezed Marilyn's elbow. She

smiled lopsidedly. "Relax, Marilyn. It's no business of mine to ruin your future. Your secret's safe with us."

"Really? You mean that?"

"I do. Take your shot at happiness. In the United States or," Ace gestured forward, "Greece, as the case may be."

Marilyn's face lit up in a sunburst of joy, but any words she might have tried to say were drowned out by a roar from the rear of the gondola. The dice game had reached a climax.

Ace called, "What's going on back there?"

Sam turned puzzled eyes forward. "Apparently, memsahib, I have won a songbird of elevated temperature."

"It couldn't have happened to a nicer fellow," Quack said, amid the laughter of all.

Bert said, "Well, that was fun, but what now?"

Ace broke into a grin. "Our next adventure can't be far off, fellas. In the meantime, we're flying. Nothing beats flying!"

THE NEW YORK HERALD

[COPYRIGHT, 1921, BY THE SUN-HERALD CORPORATION]

NEW YORK, THURSDAY, NOVEMBER 10, 1921.— ENTERED AS SECOND CLASS MATTER, POST OFFICE, NEW YORK, N. Y.

PREMIER SEE[...]
IN CONFERE[...]
PROBLEM A[...]

BRIAND ASSERTS FRA[...]
WON'T ALLOW DIC[...]
TO HER ON SIZE

Premier Insists Force Is Needed for G[...]
sian Menaces—Comes to Arms
Openminded on Pacific Questic[...]
Praise Given to Harding[...]

By RALPH [...]RTNE[...]

[Special Despatch to The New York Her[...]

Before going to dine with Secretary of Commerce the French Premier, Aristide Briand, made to T[...] his first declaration concerning the issues to be conference.

"First of all," said M. Briand, "I wish to say Washington asking nothing. In the back of our

U.S. ARMS DELEGATES
AND ADVISORY BOARD
IN FIRST CONFERENCE

Committee Named to De-
velop Organization and
Outline Scope of Duties.

AWAIT HARDING VIEWS

Keen Interest Shown in Address to Be Delivered at
Parley's Opening.

LLOYD GEORGE CABLES

Says Heart of Britain Is Deep-
ly Set on Success of the
Negotiations.

MEDAL CEREMONY CHAOS

Police Commissioner Barnaby "Dedder"
Enrich and about 50 photographers
were disappointed last night at the police
awards reception held at the Ritz Hotel.
Although slated to receive an honorary
police commission and a medal of honor,
Cecilia "Ace" Carraway failed to arrive,
and the ceremony started without her.
Photographers hoping to snap an image
of the camera-shy war hero loudly
protested her absence. Most of the
assembled into a mob and rushed the
podium.

Half those attending were police
officers, and the newshawks were soon
ejected. Afer order was restored, Dedder
awarded sixteen promotions and five
meritorious Police Duty medals to
deserving police officers.

Carraway's office would say only that
Ace was "out of town on business" and
the Herald could obtain no concrete
information on the fabled flyer's
whereabouts.

TRIO FIGHT FOR LIFE
WITH KING COBRAS

One Snake Escapes From Cage
and W[...]w H[...]lf [...]

TAMMANY'S SWEEP
IS COMPLETE IN ALL
CITY DEPARTMENTS

Hylan Plurality, $17,996;
Hulbert, 268,728 and
Craig 249,252.

NOW IN FULL CONTROL

Board of Estimate All
Democratic With 50 Ma-
jority in Aldermen.

ALL BOROUGH PRESIDENTS

Panken, Socialist, Gets Only
33,000 Against the 200,-
000 Expected.

EVERY
CK HERE

[...]l Cook
[...]n for Chat

[...]ot. 9.—Victor
[...]k in the hotel
[...]l Foch was
[...] was preparing
[...]ssenger said
[...]urs.
[...]k entered the
[...]s. The Mar-
[...]pped forward
[...]then engaged

[...]two years in
[...]nder Marshal
[...]wounded and

[...]n other cooks
[...]uld have been
[...]vercome with
[...]had to leave

[...]fended by
[...]fore Vain-

P.

147

NOTES

Dear reader, I do hope you enjoyed this installment in the *Adventures of Ace Carroway*. Here at the end, please allow me a few moments to sort reality from fiction.

Mediterranean volcanoes are quite real, although the isle of Sius is not. Sam's tales of Niatta the eater of words are, alas, entirely fictitious.

Siafu ants are real. I learned about them from aviator Beryl Markham's memoir *West with the Night*. She made history as the first pilot to cross the Atlantic Ocean against the wind in 1936, but her book poetically describes her childhood in East Africa. She faced an angry bull elephant, suffered a lion attack, and lost flesh to siafu ants. Her adventures are, if anything, more fantastic than those of Ace Carroway.

Speaking of Ace, at the close of *Growling Death* it is her intention to open an airship factory. I'm sure I won't surprise anybody when I report that she will succeed. Her first dirigible, *Sky Arrow One*, will figure prominently in her next adventure, *Ace Carroway and the Midnight Scream*, and I do hope that you will join me for the maiden voyage.

ABOUT THE AUTHOR

Wyoming native Guy Worthey traded spurs and lassos for telescopes and computers when he decided to pursue astrophysics. Whenever he temporarily escapes the gravitational pull of stars and galaxies, he writes fiction, now in the slightly less rectangular state of Washington. He plays jazz bass and happily stretches genre boundaries to find common musical ground with his classical violinist wife Diane. A beacon of inclusivity in a fractured world, he likes both cats and dogs. Creamed eggs on toast is the earthy name of his favorite food, but once in a while, he samples the celestial delights of chocolate.

ACKNOWLEDGMENTS

Especial thanks to early readers Sonya, Ryanne, and Tory. Love and gratefulness to my family, especially Diane. Everlasting gratitude to Beecher E. Strube, my high school biology teacher. Along with his partners in positivity Dana Van Burg and Terry Logue, he ran a field science program in my hometown. Poking into the surrounding forests, dunes, and fossil beds nurtured the creative spark of science in me at an impressionable age. With a twinkle in his eye and dimple in his cheek, he required that I learn to design an experiment, execute it, analyze it, and, most relevant here, write about it.

THE ADVENTURES OF ACE CARROWAY

Book 1

ACE CARROWAY AND THE GREAT WAR

Book 2

ACE CARROWAY AROUND THE WORLD

Book 3

ACE CARROWAY AND THE HANDSOME DEVIL

Book 4

ACE CARROWAY AND THE GROWLING DEATH

Book 5

ACE CARROWAY AND THE MIDNIGHT SCREAM

guyworthey.net

Made in the USA
Columbia, SC
03 May 2019